Cloud Nine

by

CARYL CHURCHILL

SAMUEL FRENCH, INC.

45 WEST 25TH STREET   NEW YORK 10010
7623 SUNSET BOULEVARD HOLLYWOOD 90046
LONDON   TORONTO

ISBN 0 573 61874 7   Printed in U.S.A.

Opening Night: May 18th, 1981

LUCILLE LORTEL'S
THEATRE DE LYS

121 Christopher Street   WA 4-8782

_____

Michel Stuart & Harvey J. Klaris
in association with
Michel Kleinman Productions

present

CLOUD 9

A New Play by
CARYL CHURCHILL

with (in alphabetical order)

DON AMENDOLIA   VERONICA CASTANG   ŽELJKO IVANEK   JEFFREY JONES
E. KATHERINE KERR   NICOLAS SUROVY   CONCETTA TOMEI

Sets by
LAWRENCE MILLER

Costumes by
MICHEL STUART & GENE LONDON

Lighting by
MARCIA MADEIRA

Title Song &
Incidental Music
MAURY YESTON

Sound by
WARREN HOGAN

Hair Supervised by
MICHAEL GOTTFRIED

Production Stage Manager
MURRAY GITLIN

General Management
WEILER/MILLER

Associate Producer
MARK BEIGELMAN

Directed by
TOMMY TUNE

CAST
(in order of appearance)

ACT I

Clive	JEFFREY JONES
Betty	ZELJKO IVANEK
Joshua	DON AMENDOLIA
Edward	CONCETTA TOMEI
Victoria	AS HERSELF
Maud	VERONICA CASTANG
Ellen/Mrs. Saunders	E. KATHERINE KERR
Harry Bagley	NICOLAS SUROVY

ACT II

Betty	E. KATHERINE KERR
Edward	JEFFREY JONES
Victoria	CONCETTA TOMEI
Martin	NICOLAS SUROVY
Lin	VERONICA CASTANG
Cathy	DON AMENDOLIA
Gerry	ZELJKO IVANEK

UNDERSTUDIES
Understudies never substitute for listed players unless a specific announcement for the appearance is made at the time of the performance.

Understudy for Men: Michael Morris, Martin Shakar
Understudy for Women: Barbara Berge

ACT I
Africa, 1880

ACT II
London, 1980

. . . but for the characters it is only 25 years later.

THERE WILL BE ONE TEN-MINUTE INTERMISSION

CLOUD NINE

ACT I

Scene 1

*(Low bright sun, Verandah, Flagpole with Union Jack, The Family—*CLIVE, BETTY, EDWARD, VIC-TORIA, MAUD, ELLEN, JOSHUA.*)*

ALL. (Sung)
> Come gather, sons of England, come gather in your pride,
> Now meet the world united, now face it side by side:
> Ye who the earth's wide corners from veldt to prairie roam
> From bush and jungle muster all
> Who call old England 'home'.
>
> Then gather round for England.
> Rally to the flag.
> From North and South and East and West
> Come one and all for England!

CLIVE.
> This is my family, though far from home

5

We serve the queen wherever we may roam,
I am a father to the natives here.
And father to my family so dear,

(HE *presents* BETTY, SHE *is played by a man*)

My wife is all I dreamt a wife should be,
And everything she is she owes to me,
BETTY.
I live for Clive, the whole aim of my life
Is to be what he looks for in a wife,
And what men want is what I want to be.

(CLIVE *presents* JOSHUA, HE *is played by a white*)

CLIVE.
My boy's a jewel, really has the knack.
You'd hardly notice that the fellow's black.
JOSHUA.
My skin is black but oh my soul is white.
I hate my tribe. My master is my light.
I only live for him. As you can see,
What white men want is what I want to be.

(CLIVE *presents* EDWARD, HE *is played by a woman*)

CLIVE.
My son is young, I'm doing all I can
To teach him to grow up to be a man.
EDWARD.
What father wants I'd dearly like to be,
I find it rather hard as you can see,

(CLIVE *presents* VICTORIA, *who is a dummy*. MAUD *and* ELLEN)

CLIVE.
No need for any speeches by the rest,
My daughter, mother-in-law, and governess.
ALL.
Then gather round for England,
Rally to the flag,
From North and South and East and West
Come one and all for England!

(ALL *go except* BETTY. CLIVE *comes*)

BETTY. Clive?
CLIVE. (BETTY.) Joshua!

(JOSHUA *comes with a drink for* CLIVE)

BETTY. I thought you would never come. The day's so long without you.

CLIVE. Long ride in the bush.

BETTY. Is anything wrong? I heard drums.

CLIVE. Nothing serious. Beauty is a damned good mare. I must get some new boots sent from home. These ones have never been right. I have a blister.

BETTY. My poor dear foot.

CLIVE. It's nothing.

BETTY. Oh but it's sore.

CLIVE. We are not in this country to enjoy ourselves. Must have ridden fifty miles. Spoke to three different headmen who would all gladly chop off each other's heads and wear them round their waists.

BETTY. Clive!

CLIVE. Don't be squeamish, Betty, let me have my joke. And what has my little dove done today?

BETTY. I've read a little.

CLIVE. Good. Is it good?

BETTY. It's poetry.

CLIVE. You're so delicate and sensitive.

BETTY. And I played the piano. Shall I send for the children?

CLIVE. Yes, in a minute. I've a piece of news for you.

BETTY. Good news?

CLIVE. You'll certainly think it's good. A visitor.

BETTY. From home?

CLIVE. No. Well of course originally from home.

BETTY. Man or women?

CLIVE. Man.

BETTY. I can't imagine.

CLIVE. Something of an explorer. Bit of a poet. Odd chap but brave as a lion. And a great admirer of yours.

BETTY. What do you mean? Whoever can it be?

CLIVE. With an H and a B. And does conjuring tricks for little Edward.

BETTY. That sounds like Mr. Bagley.

CLIVE. Harry Bagley.

BETTY. He certainly doesn't admire me, Clive, what a thing to say. How could I possibly guess from that. He's hardly explored anything at all, he's just been up a river. You should have said a heavy drinker and a bit of a bore.

CLIVE. But you like him well enough. You don't mind him coming?

BETTY. Anyone at all to break the monotony.

CLIVE. But you have your mother. You have Ellen.

BETTY. Ellen is a governess. My mother is my mother.

CLIVE. I hoped when she came to visit she would be company for you.

BETTY. I don't think mother is on a visit. I think she lives with us.

CLIVE. I think she does.

BETTY. Clive you are so good.

CLIVE. But are you bored my love?

BETTY. It's just that I miss you when you're away. We're not in this country to enjoy ourselves. If I lack society that is my form of service.

CLIVE. That's a brave girl. So today has been all right? No fainting? No hysteria?

BETTY. I have been very tranquil.

CLIVE. Ah what a haven of peace to come home to. The coolth, the calm, the beauty.

BETTY. There is one thing, Clive, if you don't mind.

CLIVE. What can I do for you my dear?

BETTY. It's about Joshua.

CLIVE. Joshua has been my boy for eight years. He has saved my life, I have saved his life. He is devoted to me and mine. I have said this before.

BETTY. He is rude to me. He doesn't do what I say. Speak to him.

CLIVE. Tell me what happened.

BETTY. He said something improper.

CLIVE. Well, what?

BETTY. I don't like to repeat it.

CLIVE. I must insist.

BETTY. I had left my book inside on the piano. I was in the hammock. I asked him to fetch it.

CLIVE. And? And did he not fetch it?

BETTY. Yes, he did eventually.

CLIVE. And what did he say?

BETTY. Clive—

CLIVE. Betty.

BETTY. He said fetch it yourself. You've got legs under that skirt.

CLIVE. Joshua!

(JOSHUA *comes*)

Joshua, madam says you spoke impolitely to her this afternoon.

JOSHUA. Sir?

CLIVE. When she asked you to pass her book from the piano.

JOSHUA. She has the book sir.

BETTY. I have the book now, but when I told you—

CLIVE. Betty, please, let me handle this. You didn't pass it at once?

JOSHUA. No, sir, I made a joke first.

CLIVE. What was that?

JOSHUA. I said my legs were tired, sir. That was funny because the book was very near, it would not make my legs tired to get it.

BETTY. That's not true.

JOSHUA. Did madam hear me wrong?

CLIVE. She heard something else.

JOSHUA. What was that, madam?

BETTY. Never mind.

CLIVE. Now, Joshua, it won't do you know. Madam doesn't like that kind of joke. You must do what Madam says, just do what she says and don't answer back. I'm very shocked, Joshua, very shocked. (CLIVE *winks at* JOSHUA *unseen by* BETTY. JOSHUA *goes*.) I think another drink, and send for the children, and isn't that Harry riding down the hill? Wave, wave. Just in time before dark. Cuts it fine, the blighter. Always a hothead, Harry.

BETTY. Can he see us?

CLIVE. Stand further forward. There, he waved back.

BETTY. Do you think so? I wonder what he saw. Sometimes sunset is so terrifying I can't bear to look.

CLIVE. It makes me proud. Elsewhere in the empire the sun is rising.

BETTY. Harry looks so small on the hillside.

(ELLEN *comes*)

ELLEN. Shall I bring the children?

BETTY. Shall Ellen bring the children?

CLIVE. Delightful.

BETTY. Yes, Ellen, make sure they're warm. The night air is deceptive. Victoria was looking pale yesterday.

CLIVE. My love.

(ELLEN *goes.* MAUD *comes from inside the house*)

MAUD. Are you warm enough Betty?

BETTY. Perfectly.

MAUD. The night air is deceptive.

BETTY. I'm quite warm. I'm too warm.

MAUD. You're not getting a fever, I hope? She's not strong, you know, Clive. I don't know how long you'll keep her in this climate.

CLIVE. I look after her majesty's domains, I think you can trust to look after my wife.

(ELLEN *comes carrying* VICTORIA, *age* 2, EDWARD *aged* 9, *lags behind*)

BETTY. Victoria, my pet, say good evening to papa.

(CLIVE *takes* VICTORIA *on his knee*)

CLIVE. There's my sweet little Vicky. What have we done today?

BETTY. She wore Ellen's hat.

CLIVE. Did she wear Ellen's big hat like a lady? What a pretty.

BETTY. And Joshua gave her a piggy back. Tell papa. Horsy with Joshy?

ELLEN. She's tired.

CLIVE. Nice Joshy played horsey. What a big strong Joshy. Did you have a gallop? Did you

make him stop and go? Not very chatty tonight
are we?

BETTY. Edward, say good evening to papa.

CLIVE. Edward my boy, have you done your lessons
well?

EDWARD. Yes papa.

CLIVE. Did you go riding?

EDWARD. Yes papa.

CLIVE. What's that you're holding?

BETTY. It's Victoria's doll. What are you doing
with it, Edward?

EDWARD. Minding her.

BETTY. Well I should give it to Ellen quickly. You
don't want papa to see you with a doll.

CLIVE. No, we had you with Victoria's doll once
before, Edward.

ELLEN. He's minding it for Vicky. He's not playing
with it.

BETTY. He's not playing with it, Clive. He's minding
it for Vicky.

CLIVE. Ellen minds Victoria, let Ellen mind the
doll.

ELLEN. Come, give it to me. (ELLEN *takes the
doll*)

EDWARD. Don't pull her about. Vicky's very fond
of her. She likes me to have her.

BETTY. He's a very good brother.

CLIVE. Yes, it's manly of you, Edward, to take
care of your little sister. We'll say no more about
it. Tomorrow I'll take you riding with me and
Harry Bagley. Would you like that?

EDWARD. Is he here?

CLIVE. He's just arrived. There Betty, take Victoria now. I must go and welcome Harry. (CLIVE *tosses* VICTORIA *to* BETTY, *who gives her to* ELLEN)

EDWARD. Can I come, Papa?

BETTY. Is he warm enough?

EDWARD. Am I warm enough?

CLIVE. Never mind the women, Ned. Come and meet Harry.

(*They go. The women are left. There is a long silence*)

MAUD. I daresay Mr. Bagley will be out all day and we'll see nothing of him.

BETTY. He plays the piano. Surely he will sometimes stay at home with us.

MAUD. We can't expect it. The men have their duties and we have ours.

BETTY. He won't have seen a piano for a year. He lives a very rough life.

ELLEN. Will it be exciting for you, Betty?

MAUD. Whatever do you mean, Ellen?

ELLEN. We don't have very much society.

BETTY. Clive is my society.

MAUD. It's time VICTORIA went to bed.

ELLEN. She'd like to stay up and see Mr. Bagley.

MAUD. Mr. Bagley can see her tomorrow.

(ELLEN *goes*)

MAUD. You let that girl forget her place, Betty.

BETTY. Mother, she is governess to my son. I

know what her place is. I think my friendship does her good. She is not very happy.

MAUD. Young women are never happy.

BETTY. Mother, what a thing to say.

MAUD. Then when they're older they look back and see that comparatively speaking they were ecstatic.

BETTY. I'm perfectly happy.

MAUD. You are looking very pretty tonight. You were such a success as a young girl. You have made a most fortunate marriage. I'm sure you will be an excellent hostess to Mr. Bagley.

BETTY. I feel quite nervous at the thought of entertaining.

MAUD. I can always advise you if I'm asked.

BETTY. What a long time they're taking. I always seem to be waiting for the men.

MAUD. Betty you have to learn to be patient. I am patient. My mama was very patient.

(CLIVE *approaches, supporting* CAROLINE SAUNDERS)

CLIVE. It is a pleasure. It is an honour. It is positively your duty to seek my help. I would be hurt. I would be insulted by any show of independence. Your husband would have been one of my dearest friends if he had lived. Betty, look who has come, Mrs. Saunders. She has ridden here all alone, amazing spirit. What will you have? Tea or something stronger? She is overcome, Betty, you will know what to do.

(MRS. SAUNDERS *sits down*)

MAUD. I knew it. I heard drums. We'll be killed in our beds.

CLIVE. Now, please, calm yourself.

MAUD. I am perfectly calm. I am just outspoken. If it comes to being killed I shall take it as calmly as anyone.

CLIVE. There is no cause for alarm. Mrs. Saunders has been alone since her husband died last year, amazing spirit. Not surprisingly the strain has told. She has come to us as her nearest neighbors.

BETTY. We are not her nearest neighbors.

CLIVE. We are among her nearest neighbors and I was a dear friend of her late husband. She knows that she will find a welcome here. She will not be disappointed. She will be cared for.

MAUD. Of course we will care for her.

BETTY. Victoria is in bed. I must go and say goodnight. Mother, please, you look after Mrs. Saunders.

CLIVE. Harry will be here at once.

(BETTY *goes*)

MAUD. How rash to go out after dark without a shawl.

CLIVE. Amazing spirit. Drink this.

MRS. S. Have you a gun? I have a gun.

CLIVE. There is no need for guns I hope. We are all friends here.

MRS. S. I think I will lie down again.

(HARRY BAGLEY *and* EDWARD *have approached.* EDWARD *is holding* HARRY's *hand.*)

MAUD. Ah, here is Mr. Bagley.

EDWARD. I gave his horse some water.

CLIVE. You don't know Mrs. Saunders, do you Harry? She has at present collapsed, but she is recovering thanks to the good offices of my wife's mother who I think you've met before. Betty will be along in a minute. Edward will go home to school shortly. He is quite a young man since you saw him.

HARRY. I hardly knew him.

MAUD. What news have you for us, Mr. Bagley?

CLIVE. Do you know Mrs. Saunders, Harry? Amazing spirit.

EDWARD. Did you hardly know me?

HARRY. Of course I knew you. I mean you have grown.

EDWARD. What do you expect?

HARRY. That's quite right, people don't get smaller.

MAUD. Edward, you should be in bed.

EDWARD. No. I'm not tired, I'm not tired am I Uncle Harry?

HARRY. I don't think he's tired.

CLIVE. He is overtired. It is past his bedtime. Say good night.

EDWARD. Goodnight, sir.

CLIVE. And to your grandmother.

EDWARD. Goodnight, grandmother.

MAUD. Shall I help Mrs. Saunders indoors? I'm afraid she may get a chill.

CLIVE. Shall I give her an arm?

MAUD. How kind of you Clive. I think I am strong enough. (MAUD *helps* MRS. SAUNDERS *into the house*)

CLIVE. Not a word to alarm the women.

HARRY. Absolutely.

CLIVE. I did some good today I think. Kept up some alliances. There's a lot of affection there.

HARRY. They're affectionate people.

CLIVE. Joshua! (*To* HARRY) I think we should sleep with guns.

HARRY. I haven't slept in a house for six months. It seems extremely safe.

(JOSHUA *comes*)

CLIVE. Joshua, you will have gathered there's being a spot of bother. You should be armed I think.

JOSHUA. There are many bad men, sir. I pray about it. Jesus will protect us.

CLIVE. He will indeed and I'll also get you a weapon. Betty, come and keep Harry company.
Look in the barn, Joshua, every night.

(CLIVE *and* JOSHUA *go*. BETTY *comes*)

HARRY. I wondered where you were.

BETTY. I was singing lullabies.

HARRY. When I think of you I always think of you with Edward in your lap.

BETTY. Do you think of me sometimes then?

HARRY. You have been thought of where no white woman has ever been thought of before.

BETTY. It's one way of having adventures. I suppose I will never go in person.

HARRY. That's up to you.

BETTY. Of course it's not. I have duties.

HARRY. Are you happy, Betty?

BETTY. Where have you been?

HARRY. Built a raft and went up the river. Stayed with some people. The king is always very good to me. They have a lot of skulls around the place but not white men's I think. I made up a poem one night. If I should die in this forsaken spot, There is a loving heart without a blot Where I will live—and so on.

BETTY. When I'm near you it's like going out into the jungle. It's like going up the river on a raft. It's like going out in the dark.

HARRY. And you are safety and light and peace and home.

BETTY. But I want to be dangerous.

HARRY. Clive is my friend.

BETTY. I am your friend.

HARRY. I don't like dangerous women.

(JOSHUA *comes, unobserved*)

BETTY. Am I dangerous?

HARRY. You are rather.

BETTY. Please like me.

HARRY. I worship you.

BETTY. Please want me.

HARRY. I don't want to want you. Of course I want you.

BETTY. What are we going to do?

HARRY. I should have stayed on the river. The hell with it. (*He takes her in his arms.* BETTY *runs off into the house.* HARRY *stays where he is. He becomes aware of* JOSHUA.)

HARRY. Who's there?

JOSHUA. Only me, sir.

HARRY. Got a gun now have you?

JOSHUA. Yes sir.

HARRY. Where's Clive?

JOSHUA. Going round the boundaries sir.

HARRY. Have you checked there's nobody in the barns?

JOSHUA. Yes sir.

HARRY. Shall we go in a barn and fuck? It's not an order.

JOSHUA. That's all right, yes.

(THEY *go off*)

ACT I

Scene 2

An open space some distance from the house.

CLIVE. Why? Why?

MRS. SAUNDERS. Don't fuss, Clive, it makes you sweat.

CLIVE. Why ride off now? Sweat, you would sweat if you were in love with somebody as disgustingly capricious as you are. You will be shot with poisoned arrows. You will miss the picnic. Somebody will notice I came after you.

MRS. SAUNDERS. I didn't want you to come after me.

CLIVE. You will be raped by cannibals.

MRS. S. I just wanted to get out of your house.

CLIVE. My God, what women put us through, Cruel, cruel, I think you are the sort of woman who would enjoy whipping somebody. I've never met one before.

MRS. S. Clive, can I tell you something?

CLIVE. Let me tell you something first. Since you came to the house I have had an erection twenty four hours a day except for ten minutes after the time we had intercourse.

MRS. S. I don't think that's physically possible.

CLIVE. You are causing me appalling physical suffering. Is this the way to treat a benefactor?

MRS. S. Clive, when I came to your house the other night I came because I was afraid. The cook was going to let his whole tribe in through the window.

CLIVE. I know that, my poor sweet. Amazing —

MRS. S. I came to you although you are not my nearest neighbour —

CLIVE. Rather than to the old major of seventy-two.

MRS. S. Because the last time he came to visit me I had to defend myself with a shotgun and I thought you would take no for an answer.

CLIVE. But you've already answered yes.

MRS. S. I answered yes once. Sometimes I want to say no.

CLIVE. Women, my God. Look, the picnic will start, I have to go to the picnic. Please Caroline—

MRS. S. I think I will have to go back to my own house.

CLIVE. Caroline, if you were shot with poisoned arrows, do you know what I'd do? I'd fuck your dead body and poison myself. Caroline, you smell

amazing. You are dark like this continent. Mysterious,
treacherous. When you rode to me through the night.
When you fainted in my arms. When I came to
you in your bed, when I lifted the mosquito netting,
when I said let me in, let me in. Oh don't shut
me out, Caroline, let me in.

(*He disappears under her skirt.*)

MRS. S. Please stop. I can't concentrate. I want
to go home. I wish I didn't enjoy the sensation because
I don't like you, Clive. I do like living in your house
where there's plenty of guns. But I don't like you
at all. But I do like the sensation. Well I'll have
it then, I'll have it.

(VOICES *are heard singing the First Noel*)

MRS. S. Don't stop. Don't stop.

(CLIVE *comes out from under* HER *skirt*)

CLIVE. The Christmas picnic. I came.
MRS. S. I didn't.
CLIVE. I'm all sticky.
MRS. S. What about me?
CLIVE. All right, are you? Come on. We mustn't
be found.
MRS. S. Don't go now.
CLIVE. Caroline, you are so voracious. Do let go.
Tidy yourself up. There's a hair in my mouth. (CLIVE
and MRS. SAUNDERS *go off.* MAUD, BETTY *enter*, JOSHUA
with a hamper.)

MAUD. I never would have thought a guinea fowl could taste so like a turkey.

BETTY. I had to explain to the cook three times.

MAUD. You did very well dear.

(JOSHUA *sits apart with gun.* EDWARD *and* HARRY *with* VICTORIA *on his shoulders, singing The First Noel.* MAUD *and* BETTY *are unpacking the hamper.* CLIVE *arrives separately*)

BETTY. Uncle Harry playing horsy.

CLIVE. And now the moment we have all been waiting for. (CLIVE *opens champagne. General acclaim*)

CLIVE. Oh dear, stained my trousers, never mind.

EDWARD. Can I have some?

MAUD. Oh no Edward, not for you.

CLIVE. Give him half a glass.

MAUD. If your father says so.

CLIVE. All rise please. To Her Majesty Queen Victoria, God bless her, and her husband and all her dear children.

ALL. The Queen.

HARRY. Excellent, Clive, wherever did you get it?

CLIVE. I know a chap in French Equatorial Africa.

(ELLEN *arrives*)

BETTY. Ellen come and play with me.

(BETTY *takes a ball from the hamper and plays catch with* ELLEN. *Murmurs of surprise and congratulations from the men whenever they catch the ball*)

EDWARD. Mama, don't play. You know you can't catch a ball.

BETTY. He's perfectly right. I can't throw either. (BETTY *sits down.* ELLEN *has the ball*)

EDWARD. Ellen, don't you play either. You're no good. You spoil it. (EDWARD *takes* VICTORIA *from* HARRY *and gives* HER *to* ELLEN. HE *takes the ball and throws it to* HARRY. HARRY, CLIVE *and* EDWARD *play ball*)

BETTY. Ellen come and sit with me. We'll be spectators and clap.

(EDWARD *misses the ball*)

CLIVE. Butterfingers.

EDWARD. I'm not.

HARRY. Throw straight now.

EDWARD. I did, I did.

CLIVE. Keep your eye on the ball.

EDWARD. You can't throw.

CLIVE. Don't be a baby.

EDWARD. I'm not, throw a hard one, throw a hard one—

CLIVE. Butterfingers. What will Uncle Harry think of you?

EDWARD. It's your fault. You can't throw. I hate you. (HE *throws the ball wildly in the direction of* JOSHUA)

CLIVE. Now you've lost the ball. He's lost the ball.

EDWARD. It's Joshua's fault. Joshua's butterfingers.

CLIVE. I don't think I want to play any more. Joshua, find the ball will you?

EDWARD. Yes, please play. I'll find the ball. Please play.

CLIVE. You're too silly and you can't catch. You'll be no good at cricket.

MAUD. Why don't we play hide and seek?

EDWARD. Because it's a baby game.

BETTY. You've hurt Edward's feelings.

CLIVE. A boy has no business having feelings.

HARRY. Hide and seek. I'll be it. Everybody must hide. This is base, you have to get home to base.

EDWARD. Hide and seek, yes.

HARRY. Can we persuade the ladies to join us?

MAUD. I'm playing. I love games.

BETTY. I always get found straight away.

ELLEN. Come on, Betty do. Vicky wants to play.

EDWARD. You won't find me ever.

(THEY *all go except* CLIVE, HARRY, JOSHUA)

HARRY. It is safe, I suppose?

CLIVE. They won't go far. This is very much my territory and it's broad daylight. Joshua will keep an open eye.

HARRY. Well I must give them a hundred. You don't know what this means to me Clive. A chap can only go on so long alone. I can climb mountains and go down rivers, but what's it for? For Christmas and England and children and women singing. This is the empire, Clive. It's not me putting a flag in new lands. It's you. The empire is one big family, I'm one of its black sheep, Clive. I know you think my life is rather dashing. But I want you to know I admire you. This is the empire, Clive, and I serve it. With all my heart.

CLIVE. I think that's about a hundred.

HARRY. Ready or not, here I come! (HE goes)

CLIVE. Harry Bagley is a fine man, Joshua. You should be proud to know him. He will be in history books.

JOSHUA. Sir, while we are alone.

CLIVE. Joshua, of course, what is it? You always have my ear. Any time.

JOSHUA. Sir, I have some information. The stable boys are not to be trusted. They whisper. They go out at night. They visit their people. Their people are not my people. I do not visit my people.

CLIVE. Thank you, Joshua. They certainly look after Beauty. I'll be sorry to have to replace them.

JOSHUA. They carry knives.

CLIVE. Thank you, Joshua.

JOSHUA. And, sir.

CLIVE. I appreciate this, Joshua, very much.

JOSHUA. Your wife.

CLIVE. Ah, yes?

JOSHUA. She also thinks Harry Bagley is a fine man.

CLIVE. Thank you, Joshua.

JOSHUA. Are you going to hide?

CLIVE. Yes, yes I am. Thank you. Keep your eyes open Joshua.

JOSHUA. I do, sir.

(CLIVE goes. JOSHUA goes. HARRY and BETTY race back to base)

BETTY. I can't run. I can't run at all.

HARRY. There, I've caught you.

BETTY. Harry, what are we going to do?

HARRY. It's impossible, Betty.

BETTY. Shall we run away together?

(MAUD *comes*)

MAUD. I give up. Don't catch me. I have been stung.

HARRY. Nothing serious I hope.

MAUD. I have ointment in my bag. I always carry ointment. I shall just sit down and rest. I'm too old for all this fun. Hadn't you better be seeking, Harry?

(HARRY *goes.* MAUD *and* BETTY *are alone for some time.* THEY *don't speak.* HARRY *and* EDWARD *race back*)

EDWARD. I won, I won, you didn't catch me.

HARRY. Yes I did.

EDWARD. Mama, who was first?

BETTY. I wasn't watching. I think it was Harry.

EDWARD. It wasn't Harry. You're no good at judging. I won, didn't I grandma?

MAUD. I expect so, since it's Christmas.

EDWARD. I won, Uncle Harry, I'm better than you.

BETTY. Why don't you help Uncle Harry look for the others.

EDWARD. Shall I?

HARRY. Yes, of course.

BETTY. Run along then. He's just coming.

(EDWARD *goes*)

BETTY. Harry, I shall scream.

HARRY. Ready or not, here I come. (HARRY *runs off*)

BETTY. Why don't you go back to the house, mother, and rest your insect bite?

MAUD. Betty, my duty is here, I don't like what I see. Clive wouldn't like it Betty. I am your mother.

BETTY. Clive gives you a home because you are my mother.

(HARRY *comes back*)

HARRY. I can't find anyone else. I'm getting quite hot.

BETTY. Sit down a minute.

HARRY. I can't do that. I'm it. How's your sting?

MAUD. It seems to be swelling up.

BETTY. Why don't you go home and rest? Joshua will go with you. Joshua!

HARRY. I could take you back.

MAUD. That would be charming.

BETTY. You can't go. You're it.

(JOSHUA *comes*)

BETTY. Joshua, my mother wants to go back to the house. Will you go with her please?

JOSHUA. Sir told me I have to keep an eye.

BETTY. I am telling you to go back to the house. Then you can come back here and keep an eye.

MAUD. Thank you Betty. I know we have our little differences, but I always want what is best for you.

(JOSHUA *and* MAUD *go*)

HARRY. Don't give way. Keep calm.

BETTY. I shall kill myself.

HARRY. Betty you are a star in my sky. Without you I would have no sense of direction. I need you, and I need you where you are. I need you to be Clive's wife. I need to go up rivers and know you are sitting here thinking of me.

BETTY. I want more than that. Is that wicked of me?

HARRY. Not wicked Betty. Silly.

(EDWARD *calls in the distance*)

EDWARD. Uncle Harry, where are you?

BETTY. Can't we ever be alone?

HARRY. You are a mother. And a daughter. And a wife.

BETTY. I think I shall go and hide again. (BETTY *goes.*)

EDWARD. Uncle Harry!

HARRY. Edward!

(EDWARD *comes*)

EDWARD. Uncle Harry! There you are. I haven't found anyone, have you?

HARRY. I wonder where they all are.

EDWARD. Perhaps they're lost forever. Perhaps they're dead. There's trouble going on isn't there, and nobody says because of not frightening the women and children.

HARRY. Yes, that's right.

EDWARD. Do you think we'll be killed in our beds?

HARRY. Not very likely.

EDWARD. I can't sleep at night. Can you?

HARRY. I'm not used to sleeping in a house.

EDWARD. If I'm awake at night can I come and see you? I won't wake you up. I'll only come if you're awake.

HARRY. You should try to sleep.

EDWARD. I don't mind being awake because I make up adventures. Once we were on a raft going down to the rapids. We've lost the paddles because we used them to fight off the crocodiles. A crocodile comes at me and I stab it again and again and the blood is everywhere and it tips up the raft and it has you by the leg and it's biting your leg right off and I take my knife and stab it in the throat and rip open its stomach and it lets go of you but it bites my hand but it's dead. And I drag you onto the river bank and I'm almost fainting with pain and we lie there in each other's arms.

HARRY. Have I lost my leg?

EDWARD. I forgot about the leg by then.

HARRY. Hadn't we better look for the others?

EDWARD. Wait, I've got something for you. It was in mama's box but she never wears it. (EDWARD *gives* HARRY *beads*) You don't have to wear it either but you might like to look at it.

HARRY. It's beautiful. But you'll have to put it back.

EDWARD. I wanted to give it to you.

HARRY. You did. It can go back in the box. You still gave it to me. Come on now, we have to find the others.

EDWARD. Harry, I love you.

HARRY. Yes I know. I love you too.

EDWARD. You know what we did when you were here before? I want to do it again. I think about it all the time. I try to do it to myself but it's not as good. Don't you want to any more?

HARRY. I do, but it's a sin and a crime and it's also wrong.

EDWARD. But we'll do it anyway won't we?

HARRY. Yes of course.

EDWARD. I wish the others would all be killed. Take it out now and let me see it.

HARRY. No.

EDWARD. Is it big now?

HARRY. Yes.

EDWARD. Let me touch it.

HARRY. No.

EDWARD. Just hold me.

HARRY. When you can't sleep.

EDWARD. We'd better find the others then. Come on.

HARRY. Ready or not, here we come. (THEY *go out with whoops and shouts.* BETTY *and* ELLEN *come*)

BETTY. Ellen, I don't want to play any more.

ELLEN. Nor do I, Betty.

BETTY. Come and sit here with me. Oh, Ellen, what will become of me?

ELLEN. Betty, are you crying? Are you laughing?

BETTY. Tell me what you think of Harry Bagley.

ELLEN. He's a very fine man.

BETTY. No, Ellen, what you really think.

ELLEN. I think you think he's very handsome.

BETTY. And don't you think he is? Oh Ellen, you're so good and I'm so wicked.

ELLEN. I'm not so good as you think.

(EDWARD *comes*)

EDWARD. I've found you.

ELLEN. We're not hiding Edward.

EDWARD. But I found you.

ELLEN. We're not playing, Edward, now run along.

EDWARD. Come on, Ellen, do play. Come on, Mama.

ELLEN. Edward, don't pull your mama like that.

BETTY. Edward, you must do what your governess says. Go and play with Uncle Harry.

EDWARD. Uncle Harry! (EDWARD *goes*)

BETTY. Ellen, can you keep a secret?

ELLEN. Oh yes, yes please.

BETTY. I love Harry Bagley. I want to go away with him. There, I've said it, it's true.

ELLEN. How do you know you love him?

BETTY. I kissed him.

ELLEN. Betty.

BETTY. He held my hand like this. Oh, I want him to do it again. I want him to stroke my hair.

ELLEN. Your lovely hair. Like this, Betty? (ELLEN *strokes* BETTY's *hair*)

BETTY. I want him to put his arm around my waist.

ELLEN. Like this, Betty?

BETTY. Yes, oh I want him to kiss me again.

ELLEN. Like this, Betty? (ELLEN *puts arm round* BETTY's *waist.*)

BETTY. Ellen, whatever are you doing? It's not a joke.

ELLEN. I'm sorry, Betty. You're so pretty. Harry

Bagley doesn't deserve you. You wouldn't really go away with him?

BETTY. Oh, Ellen, you don't know what I suffer. You don't know what love is. Everyone will hate me, but it's worth it for Harry's love.

ELLEN. I don't hate you, Betty, I love you.

BETTY. Harry says we shouldn't go away. But he says he worships me.

ELLEN. I worship you Betty.

BETTY. Oh Ellen, you are my only friend.

(THEY *embrace. The* OTHERS *have all gathered together.* MAUD *has rejoined the party, and* JOSHUA)

CLIVE. Come along, everyone, you mustn't miss Harry's conjuring trick.

MAUD. I didn't want to spoil the fun by not being here.

(BETTY *and* ELLEN *go to join the* OTHERS)

HARRY. What is it that flies all over the world and is up my sleeve? (HARRY *produces a string of union jacks from up* HIS *sleeve. General acclaim*)

CLIVE. I think we should have some singing now. Ladies, I rely on you to lead the way.

ALL. (*Sing*)
> Good King Wenceslas looked out
> On the feast of Stephen
> When the snow lay round about
> Deep and crisp and even.
> Brightly shone the moon that night
> Though the frost was cruel

When a poor man came in sight
Gathering winter fuel.

(ALL *have gone except* JOSHUA. *He sings*)

In his Master's steps he trod
Where the snow lay dinted.
Heat was in the very sod
Which the saint had printed.
Therefore Christian men be sure
Wealth or rank possessing
Ye who now do bless the poor
Shall yourselves find blessing.

ACT I

Scene 3

Inside the house. BETTY, MRS. SAUNDERS, MAUD *with* VICTORIA. *The blinds are down so the light isn't bright though it is day outside.*

MAUD. Clap hands, daddy comes, with his pockets full of plums. All for Vicky.

(CLIVE *looks in.*)

CLIVE. Everything all right? Nothing to be frightened of. Try not to listen. (CLIVE *goes. Silence*)
MRS. S. Who actually does the flogging?
MAUD. I don't think we want to imagine.

MRS. S. I imagine Joshua.

MAUD. I don't like the way you speak of it, Mrs. Saunders.

MRS. S. How should I speak of it?

MAUD. The men will do it in the proper way. They don't tell us what is going on among the tribes, and I don't think it is up to us to wonder.

MRS. S. I know a little of what is going on.

BETTY. Tell me what you know. Clive . . .

MAUD. Clive knows what is happening. Clive will know what to do. Your father always knew what to do.

(*Silence*)

MRS. S. I wonder if it's over.

(EDWARD *comes in*)

BETTY. Shouldn't you be with the men, Edward?

EDWARD. I didn't want to see any more. They got what they deserved. Uncle Harry said I could come in.

MRS. S. I never allowed the servants to be beaten in my own house. I'm going to find out what's happening. (MRS. SAUNDERS *goes out*)

BETTY. Will she go and look?

MAUD. Let Mrs. Saunders be a warning to you, Betty. She is alone in the world. You are not, thank God. Since your father died, I know what it is to be unprotected. Vicky is such a pretty little girl. Clap hands daddy comes, with his pockets full of plums. All for Vicky.

(EDWARD *is playing clap hands with* VICKY's *doll.*)

BETTY. Edward, what have you got there?

EDWARD. I'm minding her.

BETTY. Edward, I've told you before, dolls are for girls.

MAUD. Where is Ellen? She should be looking after Edward. (SHE *goes to the door*) Ellen! Betty, why do you let that girl mope about in her own room? That's not what she's come to Africa for.

BETTY. You must never let the boys at school know you like dolls. Never, never. You won't be on the cricket team, you won't grow up to be a man like your papa.

EDWARD. I don't want to be like papa. I hate papa.

MAUD. Edward! Edward!

BETTY. You're a horrid wicked boy and papa will beat you. Of course you don't hate him, you love him. Now give Victoria her doll at once.

EDWARD. She's not Victoria's doll, she's my doll. She doesn't love Victoria and Victoria doesn't love her. Victoria never even plays with her.

MAUD. Victoria will learn to play with her.

EDWARD. She's mine and she loves me and she won't be happy if you take her away, she'll cry, she'll cry, she'll cry.

(BETTY *takes the doll away, slaps him, bursts into tears.* ELLEN *comes in*)

BETTY. Ellen, look what you've done. Edward's had the doll again. Now, Ellen will you please do your job.

ELLEN. Edward, you are a wicked boy. I am going to lock you in the nursery until suppertime. Now go upstairs this minute. (SHE *slaps* EDWARD. *who bursts into tears and goes out*) I do try to do what you want. I'm so sorry. (ELLEN *bursts into tears and goes out*)

MAUD. There now, Vicky's got her baby back. Where did Vicky's naughty baby go? Shall we smack her? Just a little smack? There, now she's a good baby. Clap hands daddy comes with his pockets full of plums. All for Vicky's baby. When I was a child we honoured our parents. My mama was an angel.

(JOSHUA *comes in.* HE *stands without speakisg*)

BETTY. Joshua?

JOSHUA. Madam?

BETTY. Did you want something?

JOSHUA. Sent to see the ladies are all right, Madam.

(MRS. SAUNDERS *comes in*)

MRS. S. We're very well thank you Joshua, and how are you?

JOSHUA. Very well thank you Mrs. Saunders.

MRS. S. And the stable boys?

JOSHUA. They have had justice, Madam.

MRS. S. So I saw. And does your arm ache?

MAUD. This is not a proper conversation, Mrs. Saunders.

(HARRY *and* CLIVE *come in*)

CLIVE. Well this is all very gloomy and solemn. Can we have the shutters open? The heat of the day has gone, we could have some light, I think. And cool drinks in the gazebo, Joshua. Have some lemonade yourself. It is most refreshing.

(*Sunlight floods in as the shutters are opened.* ED-WARD *comes*)

EDWARD. Papa, papa, Ellen tried to lock me in the nursery. Mama is going to tell you of me. I'd rather tell you myself. I was playing with Vicky's doll again and I know it's very bad of me. And I said I didn't want to be like you and I said I hated you. And it's not true and I'm sorry, and please beat me and forgive me.

CLIVE. Well there's a brave boy to own up. You should always respect me and love me, Edward. Through our father we love our Queen and our God, do you understand? It is a thing men understand.

EDWARD. Yes papa.

CLIVE. Then I forgive you and shake you by the hand. You spend too much time with the women. You may spend more time with me and Uncle Harry, little man.

EDWARD. I don't like women. I don't like dolls. I love you, Papa, and I love you, Uncle Harry.

CLIVE. There's a fine fellow. Let us go out onto the gazebo.

(THEY ALL *start to go.* EDWARD *takes* HARRY'S *hand and goes with him.* CLIVE *draws* BETTY *back.*)

BETTY. Poor Clive.

CLIVE. It was my duty to have them flogged. For you and Edward and Victoria, to keep you safe.

BETTY. It is terrible to feel betrayed.

CLIVE. I sometimes feel this whole continent is my enemy. I am pitching my whole mind and will and reason and spirit against it to tame it, and it will break over me and swallow me up.

BETTY. Clive, Clive, I am here. I have faith in you.

CLIVE. Yes, I can show you my moments of weakness, Betty, because you are my wife and because I trust you. I trust you, Betty, and it would break my heart if you did not deserve that trust. Harry Bagley is my friend. It would break my heart if he did not deserve my trust.

BETTY. I'm sorry, I'm sorry. Forgive me. It is not Harry's fault, it is all mine. There is something so wicked in me Clive.

CLIVE. I have never thought of you having the weakness of your sex, only the good qualities.

BETTY. I am bad, bad, bad.

CLIVE. You are thoughtless, Betty, that's all. Women can be treacherous and evil. They are darker and more dangerous than men. The family protects us from that, you protect me from that. You are not that sort of woman. You are not unfaithful to me, Betty. I can't believe you are. It would hurt me so much to cast you off. That would be my duty.

BETTY. No, no. no.

CLIVE. Joshua has seen you kissing.

BETTY. Forgive me.

CLIVE. But I don't want to know about it. I don't want to know. It was a moment of passion such as women are too weak to resist. But you must resist it, Betty, or it will destroy us. We must fight against it. We must resist this dark female lust, Betty, or it will swallow us up.

BETTY. I do, I do resist. Help me. Forgive me.

CLIVE. Yes I do forgive you. But I can't feel the same about you as I did. You are still my wife and we still have duties to the household. (THEY *go out. As soon as* THEY *have gone* EDWARD *sneaks back to get the doll, which has been dropped on the floor.* HE *picks it up and comforts it.* JOSHUA *comes through with a tray of drinks*)

JOSHUA. Baby. Sissy. Girly. (JOSHUA *goes.* BETTY *calls from back of house*)

BETTY. Edward? (BETTY *comes in*) There you are my darling. Come, papa wants us all to be together. Uncle Harry is going to tell how he caught a crocodile. Mama's sorry she smacked you. (THEY *embrace.* JOSHUA *comes in again, passing through*) Joshua, fetch me some black thread from my sewing box. It is on the piano.

JOSHUA. You've got legs under that skirt.

BETTY. Joshua.

JOSHUA. And more than legs.

BETTY. Edward, are you going to stand there and let a servant insult your mother?

EDWARD. Joshua, get my mother's thread.

JOSHUA. Oh, little Eddy, playing at master. It's only a joke.

EDWARD. Don't you speak to my mother like that again.

JOSHUA. Ladies have no sense of humour. You like a joke with Joshua.

EDWARD. You fetch her sewing at once, do you hear me? You move when I speak to you, boy.

JOSHUA. Yes sir, Master Edward sir. (JOSHUA *goes*)

BETTY. Edward, you were wonderful. (SHE *goes to embrace* HIM *but* HE *moves away*)

EDWARD. Don't touch me.

ACT I

Scene 4

The verandah as in Scene 1. Early morning. Nobody there. JOSHUA *comes out of the house, slowly, and stands for some time doing nothing.* EDWARD *comes out.*

EDWARD. Tell me a bad story, Joshua. Nobody else is even awake yet.

JOSHUA. First there was nothing then there was the great goddess. She was very large and she had golden eyes and she made the stars and the sun and the earth. But soon she was miserable and lonely and she cried like a great waterfall and her tears made all the rivers in the world. So the great spirit sent a terrible monster, a tree with hundreds of eyes and a long green tongue, and it came chasing after her and she jumped into a lake and the tree jumped in after her, and she jumped right up into the sky. And the tree couldn't follow, he was stuck in the mud. So he picked up a big handful of mud and he threw it at her, up among the stars, and it hit her on the head. And she fell down onto earth into his arms. And the ball of mud is the moon in the sky. And then they had children which is all of us.

EDWARD. It's not true, though.

JOSHUA. Of course it's not true. It's a bad story. Adam and Eve is true. God made man white like him and gave him the bad woman who liked the snake and gave us all this trouble.

(CLIVE and HARRY come out)

CLIVE. Run along now, Edward. No, you may stay. You mustn't repeat anything you hear to your mother or your grandmother or Ellen.

EDWARD. Or Mrs. Saunders?

CLIVE. Mrs. Saunders is an unusual woman and does not require protection in the same way. Harry, there was trouble last night where we expected it. But it's all over now. Everything is under control but nobody should leave the house today I think.

HARRY. Casualties?

CLIVE. No, none of the soldiers hurt thank God. We did a certain amount of damage, set a village on fire and so forth.

HARRY. Was that necessary?

CLIVE. Obviously, it was necessary, Harry, or it wouldn't have happened. The army will come and visit, no doubt. Treat for you Edward to see the soldiers. Would you like to be a soldier?

EDWARD. I'd rather be an explorer.

CLIVE. Ah, Harry, like you see. I didn't know an explorer at his age. Breakfast, I think, Joshua. (CLIVE *and* JOSHUA *go in,* HARRY *is following*)

EDWARD. Uncle.

(HARRY *stops*)

EDWARD. Harry, why won't you talk to me?

HARRY. Of course I'll talk to you.

EDWARD. If you won't be nice to me I'll tell father.

HARRY. Edward, no, not a word, never, not to your mother, nobody, please. Edward, do you understand? Please.

EDWARD. I won't tell. I promise I'll never tell. I've cut my finger and sworn.

HARRY. There's no need to get so excited Edward. We can't be together all the time. I will have to leave soon anyway and go back to the river.

EDWARD. You can't, you can't go. Take me with you.

ELLEN. (*off*) Edward!

HARRY. I have my duty to the Empire. (HARRY *goes in.* ELLEN *comes out*)

ELLEN. Edward, breakfast time. Edward.

EDWARD. I'm not hungry.

ELLEN. Come along, Edward, for goodness sake. I'm sick of all this mooning about. I sometimes see why your parents get tired of you.

EDWARD. I'm not hungry.

ELLEN. Betty, please come and speak to Edward.

(BETTY *comes*)

BETTY. Why what's the matter?

ELLEN. He won't come in for breakfast.

BETTY. Edward, I shall call your father.

EDWARD. You can't make me eat. (HE *goes in.* BETTY *is about to follow.)*

ELLEN. Betty.

(BETTY *stops)*

ELLEN. Betty, when Edward goes to school will I have to leave?

BETTY. If you go back to England you might get married, Ellen. You're quite pretty, you shouldn't despair of getting a husband.

ELLEN. I don't want a husband. I want you.

BETTY. Children of your own, Ellen, think.

ELLEN. I don't want children, I don't like children. I just want to be alone with you, Betty, and sing for you and kiss you because I love you. I'd rather die than leave you, Betty.

BETTY. No you wouldn't, Ellen, don't be silly. Come, don't cry. You don't feel what you think you do. It's the loneliness here and the climate is very confusing. Come and have breakfast, Ellen dear, and I'll forget all about it.

(ELLEN *goes,* CLIVE *comes)*

BETTY. Clive, please forgive me.

CLIVE. Will you leave me alone?

(BETTY *goes back into the house.* HARRY *comes)*

CLIVE. Women, Harry. I envy you going off into the jungle, a man's life.

HARRY. I envy you.

CLIVE. Harry, I know you do. I have spoken to Betty.

HARRY. I assure you, Clive—

CLIVE. Please say nothing about it.

HARRY. My friendship for you—

CLIVE. Absolutely, I know the friendship between us, Harry, is not something that could be spoiled by the weaker sex. Friendship between men is a fine thing. It is the noblest form of relationship.

HARRY. I agree with you.

CLIVE. There is the necessity of reproduction. The family is all important. And there is the pleasure. But what we put ourselves through to get that pleasure, Harry. When I heard about our fine fellows last night fighting those savages to protect us I thought yes, that is what I aspire to. I tell you Harry, in confidence, I suddenly got out of Mrs. Saunders' bed and came out here on the verandah and looked at the stars.

HARRY. I couldn't sleep last night either.

CLIVE. There is something dark about women that threatens what is best in us. Between men that light burns brightly.

HARRY. I didn't know you felt like that.

CLIVE. Women are irrational, demanding, inconsistent, treacherous, lustful and they smell different from us.

HARRY. Clive—

CLIVE. Think of the comradeship of men Harry,

sharing adventures, sharing danger, risking their lives together.

(HARRY *takes hold of* CLIVE)

    CLIVE. What are you doing?
    HARRY. Well, you said—
    CLIVE. I said what?
    HARRY. Between men.

(CLIVE *is speechless*)

    HARRY. I'm sorry, I misunderstood. I would never have dreamt, I thought—
    CLIVE. My God, Harry, how disgusting.
    HARRY. You will not betray my confidence.
    CLIVE. I feel contaminated.
    HARRY. I struggle against it. You cannot imagine the shame. I have tried everything to save myself.
    CLIVE. The most revolting perversion. Rome fell Harry, and this sin can destroy an empire.
    HARRY. It is not a sin, it is a disease.
    CLIVE. A disease more dangerous than diptheria. Effeminacy is contagious. Oh Harry, how did you sink to this?
    HARRfl. Clive, help me, what am I to do?
    CLIVE. You have been away from England too long.
    HARRY. Where can I go except into the jungle to hide?
    CLIVE. You don't do it with the natives, Harry? My God, what a betrayal of the Queen.
    HARRY. Clive, I beg of you do not betray my confidence.

CLIVE. Harry, I cannot keep a secret like this. Rivers will be named after you. It's unthinkable. You must save yourself from depravity. You must get married. You are not unattractive to women. Now Mrs. Saunders. She's a woman of spirit, she could go with you on your expeditions.

HARRY. I suppose getting married wouldn't be any worse than killing myself.

CLIVE. Mrs. Saunders! Mrs. Saunders! Ask her now, Harry. Think of England.

(MRS. SAUNDERS *comes.* CLIVE *withdraws.*)

HARRY. Mrs. Saunders, will you marry me?

MRS. S. Why?

HARRY. We are both alone.

MRS. S. I choose to be alone, Mr. Bagley, If I can look after myself, I'm sure you can. Clive, I have something important to tell you. I've just found Joshua putting earth on his head. He tells me his parents were killed last night by the British soldiers. I think you owe him an apology on behalf of the Queen.

CLIVE. Joshua! Joshua!

MRS. S. Mr. Bagley, I could never be a wife again. There is only one thing about marriage that I like.

(JOSHUA *comes*)

CLIVE. Joshua, I am horrified to hear what has happened. Good God!

MRS. S. His father was shot. His mother died in the blaze. (MRS. SAUNDERS *goes*)

CLIVE. Joshua, do you want a day off? Do you

want to go to your people?

JOSHUA. Not my people, sir.

CLIVE. But you want to go to your parents' funeral?

JOSHUA. No sir.

CLIVE. Yes, Joshua, yes, your father and mother. I'm sure they were loyal to the crown. I'm sure it was all a terrible mistake.

JOSHUA. My mother and father were bad people.

CLIVE. Joshua, no.

JOSHUA. You are my father and mother.

CLIVE. Well really. I don't know what to say. That's very decent of you.

(BETTY *comes out followed by* EDWARD)

BETTY. What's the matter? What's happening?

CLIVE. Something terrible has happened. No, I mean some relatives of Joshua's met with an accident.

JOSHUA. May I go sir?

CLIVE. Yes, yes of course. Good God, what a terrible thing. Bring us a drink will you Joshua?

(JOSHUA *goes*)

EDWARD. What? What?

BETTY. Edward, go and do your lessons.

EDWARD. What is it, Uncle Harry?

HARRY. Go and do your lessons.

(ELLEN *comes out*)

ELLEN. Edward, come in here at once.

EDWARD. What's happend, uncle Harry?

HARRY. Go away. Go inside. Ellen!

ELLEN. Go inside, Edward. I shall tell your mother.

BETTY. Go inside, Edward, at once. I shall tell your father.

CLIVE. Go inside, Edward. And Betty you go inside too.

(BETTY EDWARD *and* ELLEN *go.* MAUD *comes out*)

CLIVE. Go inside. And Ellen you come outside.

(ELLEN *comes out*)

CLIVE. Mr. Bagley has something to say to you.

HARRY. Ellen, I don't suppose you would marry me?

ELLEN. What if I said yes?

CLIVE. Run along now, you two want to be alone.

(HARRY *and* ELLEN *go.* JOSHUA *brings* CLIVE *a drink*)

JOSHUA. The governess and your wife, sir.

CLIVE. What's that, Joshua?

JOSHUA. She talks of love to your wife, sir. I have seen them. Bad women.

CLIVE. Joshua, you go too far. Get out of my sight.

ACT I

Scene 5

The verandah. A table with a white cloth. A wedding cake and large knife. Bottles and glasses. JOSHUA *is putting things on the table.* EDWARD *has the doll.* JOSHUA *sees him with it.* HE *holds out* HIS *hand.* EDWARD *gives* HIM *the doll.* JOSHUA *takes the knife and cuts the doll open and shakes sawdust out of it.* JOSHUA *throws the doll under the table.*

MAUD. Come along Edward, this is such fun.

(EVERYONE *enters, making a triumphal arch for* HARRY *and* ELLEN)

MAUD. Your mama's wedding was a splended occasion, Edward. I cried and cried.

(ELLEN *takes* BETTY *aside*)

ELLEN. Betty, what happens with a man? I don't know what to do.
BETTY. You just keep still.
ELLEN. And what does he do?
BETTY. Harry will know what to do.

ELLEN. And is it enjoyable?

BETTY. Ellen, you're not getting married to enjoy yourself.

ELLEN. Don't forget me Betty.

(ELLEN *goes.*)

BETTY. I think my beads have been stolen, Clive. I did so want to wear them at the wedding.

EDWARD. It was Joshua. Joshua took them.

CLIVE. Joshua?

EDWARD. He did, he did, I saw him with them.

HARRY. Edward, that's not true.

EDWARD. It is, it is.

HARRY. Edward, I'm afraid you took them yourself.

EDWARD. I did not.

HARRY. I have seen him with them.

CLIVE. Edward, is that true? Did you take your mother's beads? And try to blame Joshua, good God.

(EDWARD *runs off*)

BETTY. Edward, come back. Have you got my beads?

HARRY. I should leave him alone. He'll bring them back.

BETTY. I wanted to wear them. I wanted to look my best at your wedding.

HARRY. You always look your best to me.

BETTY. I shall get drunk.

(MRS. SAUNDERS *comes*)

MRS. S. The sale of my property is completed.

I shall leave tomorrow. I shall go to England and buy a farm there. I shall introduce threshing machines.

CLIVE. Amazing spirit. (HE *kisses* HER. BETTY *launches herself on* MRS. SAUNDERS. *They fall to the ground.*) Betty—Caroline—I don't deserve this—Harry, Harry.

(HARRY *and* CLIVE *separate* THEM. HARRY *holding* MRS. SAUNDERS, CLIVE BETTY)

CLIVE. Mrs. Saunders, how can you abuse my hospitality? How dare you touch my wife? You must leave here at once.

BETTY. Go away, go away. You are a wicked woman.

MAUD. Mrs. Saunders, I am shocked. This is your hostess.

CLIVE. Pack your bags and leave the house this instant.

MRS. S. I was leaving anyway. There's no place for me here. I have made arrangements to leave tomorrow, and tomorrow is when I will leave. I wish you joy, Mr. Bagley. (MRS. SAUNDERS *goes*)

CLIVE. No place for her anywhere I should think. Shocking behaviour.

BETTY. Oh, Clive, forgive me, and love me like you used to.

CLIVE. Were you jealous my dove? My own dear wife!

MAUD. Ah, Mr. Bagley, one flesh, you see.

(EDWARD *comes back with the beads*)

CLIVE. Good God. Edward, it's true.

EDWARD. I was minding it for Mama because of the troubles.

CLIVE. Well done, Edward, that was very manly of you. See Betty? Edward was protecting his mama's jewels from the rebels. What a hysterical fuss over nothing. Well done, little man. It is quite safe now. The bad men are dead.

(ELLEN *comes back*)

MAUD. Ah, here's the bride. Come along, Ellen. You don't cry at your own wedding, only at other people's.

CLIVE. Now, speeches, speeches. Who is going to make a speech? Harry, make a speech.

HARRY. I'm no speaker. You're the one for that.

ALL. Speech, speech.

HARRY. My dear friends—what can I say—the empire —the family—the married state to which I have always aspired—your shining example of domestic bliss—my great good fortune in winning Ellen's love—happiest day of my life.

(*Applause*)

CLIVE. Cut the cake, cut the cake.

(HARRY *and* ELLEN *take the knife to cut the cake.* HARRY *notices the doll.*)

HARRY. What's this?

EDWARD. It was Joshua. It was Joshua.

CLIVE. Don't tell lies again. (HE *hits* EDWARD *across the side of the head*) Unaccustomed as I am to public speaking

(*Cheers*) Harry, my friend. So brave and strong and
    supple.
Ellen from neath her veil so shyly peeking.
I wish you joy. A toast—the happy couple.
Dangers are past. Our enemies are killed.
—Put your arm round her, Harry, have a kiss—
All murmuring of discontent is stilled.
Long may you live in peace and joy and bliss.

(*While* HE *is speaking.* JOSHUA *raises his gun to
shoot* CLIVE. *Only* EDWARD *sees. He does nothing
to warn the others. He puts his hands over his
ears.*)

BLACK

ACT II

OPENING (—radio announcement)

ANNOUNCER: Cloudy today with sunny periods. The high in central London twelve, that's fifty-five Fahrenheit. A really nice, mild, winter day after all that cold weather, and I for one, am going to get out into the sunshine. Traffic news if you're coming into London from the south, avoid Tower Bridge this morning, there's a half mile tail back. Otherwise, traffic's moving pretty freely into London this morning. Its 8:33, ten degrees and a nice mild day to start the week, and here to start the week . . . . . .

CLOUD NINE song on radio.

ACT II

Scene 1

Winter afternoon. VICTORIA *and* LIN, *mothers,* CATHY, LIN'S *daughter, age 4, played by a* MAN, *clinging to* LIN. VICTORIA *reading a book*

LIN. I like your shoes.
CATHY. Yum yum bubblegum
     Stick it up your mother's bum

55

When it's brown
Pull it down
Yum yum bubblegum

LIN. Cathy do stop. Do a painting.

CATHY. You do a painting.

LIN. You do a painting.

CATHY. What shall I paint?

LIN. Paint a house.

CATHY. No.

LIN. Princess.

CATHY. No.

LIN. Pirates.

CATHY. Already done that.

LIN. Spacemen.

CATHY. I never paint spacemen. You know I never.

LIN. Paint a car crash and blood everywhere.

CATHY. No, don't tell me. I know what to paint.

LIN. Go on then. You need an apron, where's an apron. Here.

CATHY. Don't want an apron.

LIN. Apron. Lift up your arms. There's a good girl.

CATHY. I don't want to paint.

LIN. Don't paint. Don't paint.

CATHY. What shall I do? You paint. What shall I do Mum?

VIC. There's nobody on the big bike, Cathy, quick.

(CATHY *goes out.* VIC *is watching the children playing outside*)

VIC. Tommy, it's Jimmy's gun. Let him have it. Don't. What the hell. (SHE *goes on reading.*

SHE *reads while she talks*)

LIN. Victoria, I don't know how you can concentrate.

VIC. You have to or you never do anything.

LIN. I suppose Tommy doesn't let you read much. I expect he talks to you while you're reading.

VIC. Yes, he does.

LIN. I didn't get very far with that book you lent me.

VIC. That's all right.

LIN. I was glad to have it, though. I sit with it on my lap while I'm watching telly. Well, Cathy's off. She's frightened I'm going to leave her. It's the baby minder didn't work out when she was two, she still remembers. You can't get them used to other people if you're by yourself. It's no good blaming me. She clings round my knees every morning up the nursery and they don't say anything but they make you feel you're making her do it. But I'm desperate for her to go to school. I did cry when I left her the first day. You wouldn't you're too fucking sensible. You'll call the teacher by her first name. I really fancy you.

VIC. What?

LIN. Put your book down will you for five minutes. You didn't hear a word I said.

VIC. I don't get much time to myself.

LIN. Do you ever go to the movies?

VIC. Tommy's very funny who he's left with. My mother babysits sometimes.

LIN. Your husband could babysit.

VIC. But then we couldn't go to the movies.

LIN. You could go to the movies with me.

VIC. Oh I see.

LIN. Couldn't you?

VIC. Well, yes, I could.

LIN. Friday night?

VIC. What film are we talking about?

LIN. Does it matter what film?

VIC. Of course it does.

LIN. You shoose then. Friday night. Not in a foreign language, ok. You don't go to the movies to read. (LIN *watches the children playing outside*)

LIN. Don't hit him, Cathy, kill him. Point the gun, kiou kiou kiou. That's the way.

VIC. They've just banned war toys in Sweden.

LIN. The kids'll just hit each other more.

VIC. Well psychologists do differ in their opinion as to whether or not aggression is innate.

LIN. Yeh?

VIC. I'm afraid I do let Tommy play with guns and just hope he'll get it out of his system and not end up in the army.

LIN. I've got a brother in the army.

VIC. Oh I'm sorry. Whereabouts is he stationed?

LIN. Belfast.

VIC. Oh dear.

LIN. I've got a friend who's Irish and we went on a Troops Out march. Now my dad won't speak to me.

VIC. I don't get on too well with my father either.

LIN. And your husband? How do you get on with him?

VIC. Oh fine. Up and down. You know. Very well. He helps with the washing up and everything.

LIN. I left mine two years ago. He let me keep

Cathy and I'm grateful for that.

VIC. You shouldn't be grateful.

LIN. I'm a lesbian.

VIC. You still shouldn't be grateful.

LIN. I'm grateful he didn't hit me harder than he did.

VIC. I suppose I'm very lucky with Martin.

LIN. Don't get at me about how I bring up Cathy, OK?

VIC. I didn't.

LIN. Yes you did. War toys. I'll give her a rifle for Christmas and blast Tommy's pretty head off for a start.

(VIC *goes back to* HER *book*)

LIN. I hate men.

VIC. You have to look at it in a historical perspective in terms of learnt behavior since the industrial revolution.

LIN. I just hate the bastards.

VIC. Well, it's a point of view.

(CATHY *has come back meanwhile and started painting.* EDWARD *comes in.*)

(EDWARD *comes in*)

EDWARD. Victoria. Vic. Mother's here, in the park. She's walking round all the paths very fast.

VIC. By herself?

EDWARD. I told her you were here.

VIC. Thanks.

EDWARD. Come on.

VIC. Ten minutes talking to my mother and I have to spend two hours in a hot bath. (VIC *goes out*)

LIN. You're gay aren't you? I really fancy your sister. I thought you'd understand. You do but you can go on pretending you don't. I don't mind. Shit, Cathy. what about an apron. I don't mind you having paint on your clothes but if it doesn't wash off just don't tell me you can't wear your dress with paint on, O.K.?

CATHY. O.K.

EDWARD. Don't go around saying that. I might lose my job.

LIN. That last gardener was ever so straight. He used to flash at all the little girls.

EDWARD. I wish you hadn't said that about me. It's not true.

LIN. It's not true and I never said it and I never thought it and I never will think it again.

EDWARD. Someone might have heard you.

LIN. Shut up about it then.

(BETTY *and* VICTORIA *come up*)

BETTY. It's quite a nasty bump.

VIC. He's not even crying.

BETTY. I think that's very worrying. You and Edward always cried. Perhaps he's got concussion.

VIC. Of course he hasn't mummy.

BETTY. That other little boy was very rough. Should you speak to somebody about him?

VIC. Tommy was hitting him with a spade.

BETTY. Well he's a real little boy. And so brave
not to cry. You must watch him for signs of drowsi-
ness. And nausea. If he's sick in the night, phone
an ambulance. Well, you're looking very well, darling,
a bit tired, a bit peaky. I think the fresh air
agrees with Edward. He likes the open air life
because of growing up in Africa. He misses the
sunshine don't you darling? We'll soon have Edward back on his feet. What fun it is here.

VIC. This is Lin. And Cathy.

BETTY. Oh Cathy what a lovely painting. What
is it? Well I think it's a house on fire. I think
all that red is a fire. Is that right? Or do I see
legs, is it a horse? Can I have the lovely painting
or is it for mummy? Children have such imagination,
it makes them so exhausting. (To LIN) I'm sure
you're wonderful, just like Victoria. I had help with
my children. One does need help. That was in Africa
of course so there wasn't the servant problem. This
is my son Edward. This is—

EDWARD. Lin.

BETTY. Lin, this is Lin. Edward is doing something
such fun, he's working in the park as a gardener.
He does look exactly like a gardener.

EWADRD. I am a gardener.

BETTY. He's certainly making a stab at it. Well
it will be a story to tell. I expect he will write
a novel about it, or perhaps a television series.
Well what a pretty child, Victoria was a pretty
child just like a little doll—You can't be certain
how they'll grow up. I think Victoria's very pretty
but she doesn't make the most of herself, do you
darling, it's not the fashion I'm told but there are

still women who read Vogue, well we hope that's
not what Martin looks for, though in many ways
I wish it was. I don't know what it is Martin looks
for and nor does he I'm afraid poor Martin. Well
I am rattling on. I like your blouse dear but your
shoes won't do at all. Well do they have lady gardeners, Edward, because I'm going to leave your father
and I think I might need to get a job, not a gardener
really of course. I haven't got green fingers I'm
afraid, everything I touch shrivels straight up. Vicky
gave me a poinsettia last Christmas and the leaves
all fell off on Boxing Day. Well good heavens, look
what's happened to that lovely painting.

(CATHY *has slowly and carefully been going over
the whole sheet with black paint.*)

LIN. What do you do that for silly? It was
nice

CATHY. I like your earrings.

BETTY. Do you darling?

VIC. Did you say you're leaving Daddy?

BETTY. Shall I put them on you? My ears aren't
pierced, I never wanted that, they clip on the lobe.

LIN. She'll get paint on you, mind.

BETTY. There's a pretty girl. It doesn't hurt does
it? Well you'll grow up to know you have to suffer
a little bit for beauty.

CATHY. Look mum I'm pretty. I'm pretty, I'm
pretty.

LIN. Stop showing off Cathy.

VIC. It's time we went home, Tommy, time to
go home. Last go then, all right.

EDWARD. Mum, did I hear you right just now?

CATHY. I want my ears pierced.

BETTY. Ooh, not till you're big.

CATHY. I know a girl got her ears pierced and she's three. She's got real gold.

BETTY. I don't expect she's English, darling. Can I give her a sweety? I know they're not very good for the teeth. Vicky gets terribly cross with me. What does mummy say?

LIN. Just one, thank you very much.

CATHY. I like your beads.

BETTY. Yes, they are pretty. Here you are.

LIN. Don't get paint on it.

CATHY. Look at me, look at me. Vicky, Vicky, Vicky look at me.

LIN. You look lovely, come on now.

CATHY. And your hat, and your hat.

LIN. No, that's enough.

BETTY. Of course she can have my hat.

CATHY. Yes, yes, hat hat.

EDWARD. There, get it straight.

CATHY. Look look look.

LIN. That's enough, please, stop it now. Hat off, bye bye hat.

CATHY. Give me my hat.

LIN. Bye bye beads.

BETTY. It's just fun.

LIN. It's very nice of you.

CATHY. I want my beads.

LIN. Where's the other earring?

CATHY. I want my beads.

LIN. You'll have a smack.

BETTY. Have you got the earring?

CATHY. I want my beads.

BETTY. Thank you darling.

CATHY. I want my beads, you're horrid, I hate you, mum, you smell.

BETTY. This is the point you see where one had help. Well it's been lovely seeing you dears and I'll be off again on my little walk.

VIC. You're leaving him? Really?

BETTY. Yes you heard aright Vicky, yes, I'm finding a little flat, that will be fun. (BETTY *goes*) Bye bye Tommy granny's going now. Tommy don't hit that little girl, say goodbye to granny.

VIC. Fucking hell.

EDWARD. Puking Jesus.

LIN. That was news was it, leaving your father?

EDWARD. They're going to want so much attention.

VIC. Does everybody hate their mothers?

EDWARD. Mind you, I wouldn't live with him.

LIN. Stop sniveling, pigface. Where's your scarf? Be quiet now and we'll have doughnuts for tea and if you keep on we'll have dogshit on toast.

VIC. Tommy, you've had two last goes. Last last last last go.

LIN. Not that funny, come on, scarf on.

EDWARD. Can I have your painting?

CATHY. What for?

EDWARD. For a friend of mine.

CATHY. What's his name?

EDWARD. Gerry.

CATHY. How old is he?

EDWARD. Twenty-five.

CATHY. You can if you like. I don't care. Kiou

kiou kiou kiou. (CATHY *goes out.* EDWARD *takes the painting and goes out*)

LIN. Will you have sex with me?

VIC. I don't know what Martin would say. Does it count as adultery with a woman?

LIN. You'd enjoy it.

ACT II

Scene 2

Spring. EDWARD *is gardening.*

GERRY. Eddie, come and sit down. (*to audience*) Two years I've been with Edward.

EDWARD. If the superintendent comes I'll be in trouble. It's not my dinnertime yet. Sometimes I pretend we don't know each other and you've come to the park to eat your lunch and look at me.

GERRY. That would be more interesting, yes.

EDWARD. Where were you last night? I think you owe me an explanation. We always do tell each other everything.

GERRY. Is that a rule?

EDWARD. It's what we agreed.

GERRY. It's a habit we've got into. Look, I was drunk. I woke up at 4 o'clock on somebody's floor. I was sick. I hadn't any money for a cab. I went back to sleep.

EDWARD. You could have phoned.

GERRY. There wasn't a phone.

EDWARD. Sorry.

GERRY. There was a phone and I didn't phone you. Leave it alone, Eddy, I'm warning you.

EDWARD. What are you going to do to me then?

GDRRY. I'm going to the pub.

EDWARD. I'll join you in ten minutes.

GERRY. I didn't ask you to come. (*to audience*) You have to get away sometimes or you lose sight of yourself. The train from Victoria to Clapham is one of the old type. Separate compartments, no connecting corridor, so once the train starts no one can get in or out until the next station. As soon as I got on the platform I saw who I wanted. Slim hips, tense shoulders, trying not to look at anyone. I put my hand on my packet just long enough so he couldn't miss it. The train came in. You don't want to get in too fast or some straight dumbo might get in with you. I stay by the window. I couldn't see where the fuck he'd got to. Then just as the whistle went he got in. Great. It's a six-minute journey so you can't start anything you can't finish. I stared at him and he unzipped his flies. Then he stopped. So I stood up and took my cock out. He took me in his mouth and shut his eyes tight. He was sort of mumbling it about as if he wasn't sure what to do, so I said, "A bit tighter son" and he said "Sorry" and then got on with it. He was jerking off with his left hand, and I could see he's got a fair-sized one. I wished he'd keep still so I could see his watch. I was getting really turned on. What if we pulled into

Clapham Junction now. Of course by the time we sat down again the train was just slowing up. I felt wonderful. Then he started talking. It's better if nothing is said. Once you find he's a librarian in Walthamstow with a special interest in science fiction and lives with his aunt, then forget it. He said I hope you don't think I do this all the time. I said I hope you will from now on. He said he would if I was on the train, but why don't we go out for a meal? I opened the door before the train stopped. I told him I live with somebody, I don't want to know. He was jogging sideways to keep up. He said "what's your phone number, you're my ideal physical type, what sign of the zodiac are you? Where do you live? Where are you going now? It's not fair." I saw him at Victoria a couple of months later and I went straight down to the end of the platform and I picked up somebody really great who never said a word. Just smiled.

(GERRY *goes.* CATHY *comes.*)

CATHY.
  Batman and Robin
  Had a batmobile
  Robin done a fart
  And paralyzed the wheel
  The wheel couldn't take it
  The engine fell apart
  All because of Robin
  And his supersonic fart

(CATHY *goes.* MARTIN, VICTORIA *and* BETTY *walking slowly*)

(MARTIN, VICTORIA *and* BETTY *walking slowly*)

MARTIN. Tom!

BETTY. He'll fall in.

VIC. No he won't.

MARTIN. Don't go too near the edge Tom. Throw the bread from there. The ducks can get it.

BETTY. I'll never be able to manage. If I can't even walk down the street by myself. Everything looks so fierce.

VIC. Just watch Tommy feeding the ducks.

BETTY. He's going to fall in. Make Martin make him move back.

VIC. He's not going to fall in.

BETTY. It's since I left your father.

VIC. Mummy, it really was the right decision.

BETTY. Everything comes at me from all directions. Martin despises me.

VIC. Of course he doesn't mummy.

BETTY. Of course he does.

MARTIN. Throw the bread. That's the way. The duck can get it. Quack quack quack quack quack.

BETTY. I don't want to take pills. Lin says you can't trust doctors.

VIC. You're not taking pills. You're doing very well.

BETTY. But I'm so frightened.

VIC. What are you frightened of?

BETTY. Victoria, you always ask that as if there was suddenly going to be an answer.

VIC. Are you all right sitting there?

(VICTORIA *joins* MARTIN. BETTY *stays sitting on the bench.*)

MARTIN. You take the job, you go to Manchester. You turn it down, you stay in London. People are making decisions like this every day of the week. It needn't be for more than a year. You get long vacations. Our relationship might well stand the strain of that, and if it doesn't we're better out of it. I don't want to put any pressure on you. I'd just like to know so we can sell the house. I think we're moving into an entirely different way of life if you go to Manchester because it won't end there. We could keep the house as security for Tommy, but he might as well get used to the fact that life nowadays is insecure. You should ask your mother what she thinks and then do the opposite. I could just take that room in Barbara's house, and then we could babysit for each other. You think that means I want to fuck Barbara. I don't. Well, I do, but I won't. And even if I did, what's a fuck between friends? What are we meant to do it with, strangers? Whatever you want to do, I'll be delighted. If you could just let me know what it is I'm to be delighted about. Don't cry again, Vicky, I'm not the sort of man who makes women cry.

(LIN *has come in, and sat down with* BETTY. CATHY *joins them;* SHE *is wearing a pink dress, has holster with pistol*)

LIN. I've brought her three new frocks. She won't wear jeans to school any more because Tracy and Mandy called her a boy.

CATHY. Tracy's got a perm.

LIN. You should have shot them.

CATHY. They're coming to tea and we've got to have trifle. Not trifle you make, trifle out of a packet. And you've got to wear a skirt. And tights.

LIN. Tracy's mum wears jeans.

CATHY. She does not. She wears velvet.

BETTY. Well I think your mummy looks very pretty. And if that gun has caps in it please take it a long way away.

CATHY. It's got red caps. They're louder.

MARTIN. Do you think you're well enough to do this job. You don't have to do it. No one's going to think any the less of you if you stay here with me. There's no point being so liberated you make yourself cry all the time. You stay and we'll get everything sorted out. What it is about sex, when we talk while it's happening I get to feel it's like a driving lesson. Left, right, a little faster, carry on, slow down . . .

(CATHY *shoots* VICTORIA)

CATHY. You're dead Vicky.

VIC. Aaargh.

CATHY. Fall over.

VIC. Yes, I'm dead.

CATHY. The Dead Hand Gang fall over. They said I had to fall over in the mud or I can't play. That duck's a mandarin.

MARTIN. Which one? Look, Tommy.

CATHY. That's a diver. It's got a yellow eye and it dives. That's a goose. Tommy doesn't know it's a goose, he thinks it's a duck. The babies get eaten by weasels. Kiou kiou.

(CATHY *goes off*)

MARTIN. So, I lost my erection last night not because I'm not prepared to talk, it's just that taking in technical information is a different part of the brain and also I don't like to feel that you do it better to yourself. I have read the Hite report. I do know that women have to learn to get their pleasure despite our clumsy attempts at expressing undying devotion and ecstasy, and that what we spent our adolescence thinking was an animal urge we had to suppress is in fact a fine art we have to acquire. I'm not like whatever percentage of American men have become impotent as a direct result of women's liberation, which I am totally in favor of, more I sometimes think than you are yourself. Nor am I one of your villains who sticks it in, bangs away, and falls asleep. My one aim is to give you pleasure. My one aim is to give you rolling orgasms like I do other women. So why the hell don't you have them? My analysis for what it's worth is that despite all my efforts you still feel dominated by me. I in fact think it's very sad that you don't feel able to take that job. It makes me feel very guilty. I don't want you to do it because I encourage you to do it. But don't you think you'd feel better if you did take the job? You're the one who's talked about freedom. You're the one who's experimenting with bisexuality, and I don't stop you, I think women have something to give each other. You seem to need the mutual support. You find me too over-whelming. So follow it through, go away, leave me and Tommy alone for a bit, we can manage perfectly well without you. I'm not putting any pressure on you but I don't think you're being a whole person. God knows I do everything I can to make you stand on you own two feet. Just be yourself. You don't seem to realize how insulting it is to me that you can't get yourself together.

(MARTIN *and* VIC *come back.*)

BETTY. You must be very lonely yourself with no husband. You don't miss him?

LIN. Not really, no.

BETTY. Maybe you like being on your own.

LIN. I'm seeing quite a lot of Vicky. I don't live alone. I live with Cathy.

BETTY. I would have been frightened when I was your age. I thought, the poor children, their mother all alone.

LIN. I've a lot of friends.

BETTY. I find when I'm making tea I put out two cups. It's strange not having a man in the house. You don't know who to do things for.

LIN. Yourself.

BETTY. Oh, that's very selfish.

LIN. Have you any women friends?

BETTY. I've never been so short of men's company that I've had to bother with women.

LIN. Don't you like women?

BETTY. They don't have such interesting conversations as men. There has never been a woman composer of genius. They don't have a sense of humor. They spoil things for themselves with their emotions. I can't say I do like women very much no.

LIN. But you're a woman.

BETTY. There's nothing says you have to like yourself.

LIN. Do you like me?

BETTY. There's no need to take it personally. Lin.

(MARTIN *and* VIC *come back.*)

MARTIN. Did you know if you put cocaine on your prick you can keep it up all night? The only thing is of course it goes numb so you don't feel anything. But you would, that's the main thing. I just want to make you happy.

BETTY. Vicky I'd like to go home.

VIC. Yes, mummy, of course.

BETTY. I'm sorry dear.

VIC. I think Tommy would like to stay out a bit longer.

LIN. Hello, Martin. We do keep out of each other's way.

MARTIN. I think that's the best thing to do.

BETTY. Perhaps you'd walk home with me. Martin. I do feel safer with a man. The park is so large the grass seems to tilt.

MARTIN. Yes, I'd like to go home and do some work. I'm writing a novel about women from the women's point of view.

(MARTIN *and* BETTY *go.* LIN *and* VIC *are alone*
    THEY *embrace*)

VIC. Why the hell can't he just be a wife and come with me? Why does Martin make me tie myself in knots? No wonder we can't just have a simple fuck. No, not Martin, why do I make myself tie myself in knots. It's got to stop, Lin. I'm not like that with you. Would you love me if I went to Manchester?

LIN. Yes.

VIC. Would you love me if I went on a climbing expedition in the Andes mountains?

LIN. Yes.

VIC. Would you love me if my teeth fell out?

LIN. Yes.

VIC. Would you love me if I loved ten other people?

LIN. And me?

VIC. Yes.

LIN. Yes.

VIC. And I feel apologetic for not being quite so subordinate as I was. I am more intelligent than him. I am brilliant.

LIN. Leave him Vic, come and live with me.

VIC. Don't be silly.

LIN. Silly, Christ, don't then. I'm not asking because I need to live with somene I would enjoy it, that's all, we'd both enjoy it. Cathy, for fuck's sake stop throwing stones at the ducks. The man's going to get you.

VIC. What man? Do you need a man to frighten your child with?

LIN. My mother said it.

VIC. You're so inconsistent, Lin.

LIN. I've changed who I sleep with. I can't change everything.

VIC. Like when I had to stop you getting a job in a boutique and collaborating with sexist consumersim.

LIN. I should have got that job. Cathy would have liked it. Why shouldn't I have some decent clothes? I'm sick of dressing like a boy, why can't I look sexy, wouldn't you love me?

VIC. Lin, you've no analysis.

LIN. No but I'm good at kissing aren't I? I give Cathy guns, my mum didn't give me guns. I dress her in jeans, she wants to wear dresses, maybe she should wear dresses. I don't know. I can't work it out. I don't want to. You read too many books, you get at me all the time, you're worse to me than Martin is to you, you piss me off, my brother's been killed. I'm sorry to win the argument that way but there it is.

VIC. What do you mean win the argument?

LIN. I mean be nice to me.

VIC. In Belfast?

LIN. I heard this morning. Don't, don't start. I've hardly seen him for two years. I rung my father. You'd think I'd shot him myself. He doesn't want me to go to the funeral.

VIC. What will you do?

LIN. Go of course.

CATHY. What is it? Who's killed? What?

LIN. It's Bill. Your uncle. In the army. Bill what give you the blue teddy.

CATHY. Can I have his gun?

LIN. It's time we went home. Time you went to bed.

CATHY. No it's not.

LIN. We go home and you have tea and you have a bath and you go to bed.

CATHY. Fuck off.

LIN. Cathy shut up.

VIC. It's only half past five why don't we—

LIN. I'll tell you why she has to go to bed—

VIC. She can come home with me.

LIN. Because I want her out the fucking way.

VIC. She can come home with me.

CATHY. I'm not going to bed.

LIN. I want her home with me not home with you. I want her in bed. I want today over.

CATHY. I'm not going to bed.

(LIN *hits* CATHY, CATHY *cries*)

LIN. I'll give you something to cry for.

CATHY. I'm not going to bed.

VIC. Cathy—

LIN. You keep out of it.

VIC. Lin for God's sake.

(THEY *are all shouting.* CATHY *runs off.* LIN *and* VIC *are silent. They embrace.*)

LIN. Where's Tommy?

VIC. Didn't he go with Martin?

LIN. Did he?

VIC. God oh God.

LIN. Cathy! Cathy!

VIC. I haven't thought about him. How could I not think about him? Tommy.

LIN. Cathy! Come on, quick, I want some help.

VIC. Tommy! Tommy!

(CATHY *comes back*)

LIN. Where's Tommy? Did he go with Martin? Do you know where he is?

CATHY. I showed him the goose. We went in the bushes.

LIN. Then what?

CATHY. I came back on the swing.

VIC. And Tommy? Where was Tommy?

CATHY. He fed the ducks.

LIN. No that was before.

CATHY. He did a pee in the bushes. I helped him with his trousers.

VIC. And after that?

CATHY. He fed the ducks.

VIC. No no.

CATHY. He liked the ducks. I expect he fell in.

LIN. Did you see him fall in?

VIC. Tommy! Tommy!

LIN. What's the last time you saw him?

CATHY. He did a pee.

VIC. Mummy said he would fall in. Oh, God, Tommy!

LIN. We'll go round the pond. We'll go opposite ways round the pond.

ALL. (*Shout*) Tommy!

(VIC *and* LIN *go off opposite sides.* CATHY *climbs on the bench.*)

CATHY.
    Georgy Best superstar.
    walks like a woman and wears a bra,
    There is is! I see him! Mum! Vicky! There
he is! He's in the bushes.
    LIN. (*Comes back*) Come on, Cathy love, let's
go home.
    CATHY. Vicky's got him.
    LIN. Come on.
    CATHY. Is she cross?
    LIN. No, come on.
    CATHY. I found him.
    LIN. Yes. Come on.

(LIN *and* CATHY *hug.*)

    CATHY. I'm watching telly.
    LIN. OK.
    CATHY. After the news.
    LIN. OK.
    CATHY. I'm not going to bed.
    LIN. Yes you are.
    CATHY. I'm not going to bed now.
    LIN. Not now but early.
    CATHY. How early?
    LIN. Not late.
    CATHY. How not late?
    LIN. Early.
    CATHY. How early?
    LIN. Not late. (THEY *go off together.* GERRY *comes on.* HE *waits.* EDWARD *comes.* HE *has changed out of* HIS *work clothes*)

EDWARD. I've got some fish for dinner. I thought I'd make a cheese sauce.

GERRY. I won't be in.

EDWARD. Where are you going?

GERRY. For a start I'm going to a sauna. Then I'll see.

EDWARD. All right. What time will you be back? We'll eat then.

GERRY. You're getting like a wife.

EDWARD. I don't mind that.

GERRY. Why don't I do the cooking sometime?

EDWARD. You can if you like. You're just not so good at it that's all. Do it tonight.

GERRY. I won't be in tonight.

EDWARD. Do it tomorrow. If we can't eat it we can always go to a restaurant.

GERRY. Stop it.

EDWARD. Stop what?

GERRY. Just be yourself.

EDWARD. I don't know what you mean. Everyone's always tried to stop me being feminine and now you are too.

GERRY. You're putting it on.

EDWARD. I like doing the cooking. I like being fucked. You do like me like this really.

GERRY. I'm bored Eddy.

EDWARD. Go to the sauna.

GERRY. And you'll stay home and wait up for me.

EDWARD. No, I'll go to bed and read a book.

GERRY. Or knit. You can knit me a pair of socks—

EDWARD. I might knit. I like knitting.

GERRY. I don't mind if you knit. I don't want to be married.

EDWARD. I do.

GERRY. Well I'm divorcing you.

EDWARD. I wouldn't want to keep a man who wants his freedom.

GERRY. Eddy, do stop playing the injured wife, it's not funny.

EDWARD. I'm not playing. It's true.

GERRY. I'm not the husband so you can't be the wife.

EDWARD. I'll always be here, Gerry, if you want to come back. I know you men like to go off by yourselves. I don't think I could love deeply more than once. But I don't think I can face life on my own so don't leave it too long or it may be too late.

GERRY. What are you trying to turn me into?

EDWARD. A monster, darling, which is what you are.

GERRY. I'll collect my stuff from the flat in the morning. (GERRY *goes.* EDWARD *sits on the bench. It gets darker.* VICTORIA *comes*)

VIC. Martin's reading Tommy a story. Isn't it quiet. (THEY *sit on the bench, holding hands*)

EDWARD. I like women.

VIC. That should please mother.

EDWARD. No listen Vicky. I'd rather be a woman. I wish I had breasts like that, I think they're beautiful. Can I touch them?

VIC. What, pretending they're yours?

EDWARD. No, I know it's you.

VIC. I think I should warn you I'm enjoying this.

EDWARD. I'm sick of men.

VIC. I'm sick of men.

EDWARD. I think I'm a lesbian.

ACT II

Scene 3

Another part of the park. Summer night. VICTORIA, LIN *and* EDWARD *enter with quilt and bottle of wine.*

LIN. Where are you?

VIC. Come on.

EDWARD. Do we sit in a circle?

VIC. No, kneel down and face north.

EDWARD. Lost my compass.

VIC. Give me your hand. We all hold hands.

EDWARD. Do you know what to do?

LIN. She's making it up.

VIC. We start off by being quiet.

EDWARD. What?

LIN. Hush.

EDWARD. Will something appear?

VIC. It was your idea.

EDWARD. It wasn't my idea. It was your book.

LIN. You said call up the goddess.

EDWARD. I don't remember saying that.

LIN. We could have called her on the telephone.

EDWARD. Come on, Lin, this is meant to be serious.

VIC. Innin. Innana. Nana. Nut. Anat. Anahita. Istar. Isis.

LIN. I can't remember all that.

VIC. Lin! Innin, Innana, Nana, Nut, Anat, Anahita, Istar, Isis—(ALL *repeat Innin etc.*) Goddess hear us calling you back through time, hear us, Lady, give us back what we were, give us the history we haven't had, make us the women we can't be.

LIN. Come back, goddess.

VIC. Goddess of the sun and the moon her brother, little goddess of Crete with snakes in your hands.

LIN. Goddess of breasts.

VIC. Goddess of cunts.

LIN. Goddess of fat bellies and babies.

LIN. And blood.

(ALL *repeat Innin, etc.*)

LIN. I see her.

EDWARD. What?

LIN. I see her. Very tall. Snakes in her hands. Light light light—Look out! Did I give you a fright?

EDWARD. I was terrified.

VIC. Don't spoil it Lin.

LIN. It's all out of a book.

VIC. Innin,—I can't do it now. I was really enjoying myself.

LIN. She won't appear with a man here.

VIC. They had men, they had sons and lovers.

EDWARD. They had eunuchs.

LIN. Don't give us ideas.

VIC. There's Attis and Tammuz, they're torn to pieces.

EDWARD. Tear me to pieces, Lin.

VIC. The priestess chose a lover for a year and he was king because she chose him and then he was killed at the end of the year. And the women had the children and nobody knew it was done by fucking so they didn't know about fathers and nobody cared who the father was and the property was passed down through the maternal line—

LIN. Don't turn it into a lecture, Vicky, it's meant to be an orgy.

VIC. It never hurts to understand the theoretical background. You can't separate fucking and economics.

LIN. Give us a kiss.

EDWARD. Shut up, listen.

LIN. What?

EDWARD. There's somebody there.

LIN. Where?

EDWARD. There.

VIC. The priestesses used to make love to total strangers.

LIN. Go on then, I dare you.

EDWARD. Go on, Vicky.

VIC. He won't know it's a sacred rite in honour of the goddess.

EDWARD. We'll know.

LIN. We can tell him.

EDWARD. It's not what he thinks, it's what we think.

LIN. Don't tell him till after, he'll run a mile.

VIC. Hello. We're having an orgy. Do you want me to suck your cock?

(*The stranger approaches. It is* MARTIN)

MARTIN. There you are. I've been looking everywhere. What the hell are you doing? Do you know what the time is? You're all pissed out of your minds.

(THEY *leap on* MARTIN, *pull* HIM *down and caress him.*)

(*Another stranger approaches*)

MARTIN. Well that's all right. If all we're talking about is having a lot of sex there's no problem. I was all for the sixties when liberation just meant fucking.

LIN. Hey you, come here. Come and have sex with us.

VIC. Who is it?

LIN. It's my brother.

EDWARD. Lin, don't.

LIN. It's my brother.

VIC. It's her sense of humour, you get used to it.

LIN. Shut up Vicky, it's my brother. Isn't it? Bill?

SOLDIER. Yes it's me.

LIN. And you are dead.

SOLDIER. Fucking dead all right yeh.

LIN. Have you come back to tell us something?

SOLDIER. No I've come for a fuck. That was the worst thing in the fucking army. Never fucking let out. Can't fucking talk to Irish girls. Fucking bored out of my fucking head. That or shit scared. For five minutes I'd be glad I wasn't bored. Then I was fucking scared. Then we'd come in and I'd

be glad I wasn't scared and then I was fucking
bored. Spent the day reading fucking porn and
the fucking night wanking. Man's fucking life in
the fucking army? No fun when the fucking kids
hate you. I got so I fucking wanted to kill someone
and I got fucking killed myself and I want a fuck.

LIN. I miss you. Bill Bill. (LIN *collapses*, SOL-
DIER *goes*. VIC *comforts* LIN)

EDWARD. Let's go home.

LIN. Vic, come home with us. Vic's coming to
live with me and Edward.

MARTIN. Tell me about it in the morning.

LIN. Its true.

VIC. It is true.

MARTIN. Tell me when you're sober.

(LIN, EDWARD *and* VIC *go off*. GERRY *comes on*)

GERRY. I come here sometimes at night and pick
somebody up. Sometimes I come here at night and
don't pick anybody up. I do also enjoy walking
about at night. There's never any trouble finding
someone. I can have sex any time. You might not
find the type you most fancy every day of the
week, but there's plenty of people who just enjoy
having a good time.

(MARTIN *goes off*)

GERRY. I quite like living alone. If I live with someone
I get annoyed with them. Edward always put on
Capital radio when he got up. The silence gets wasted.

I wake up at four o'clock sometimes. Birds. Silence. If I bring somebody home I never let them stay the night.

HARRY. (*From Act I, off stage*) Edward!

GERRY. Edward, Edward.

EDWARD. (*From Act I*) There you are. I haven't found anyone have you?

GERRY. I can't sleep at night.

EDWARD. I don't mind being awake because I make up adventures. You know what we did before? I want to do it again, I think about it all the time. Don't you want to any more?

GERRY. Just hold me.

HARRY. (*From Act I, off stage*) Edward!

EDWARD. When you can't sleep. (EDWARD *goes off*)

ACT II

Scene 4

Afternoon in late summer. MARTIN, CATHY, EDWARD.

EDWARD. You'll have Tommy and Cathy tonight then OK? Tommy's still on antibiotic, do make him finish the bottle, he takes it in Ribena. It's no good in orange, he spits it out. Remind me to give you Cathy's swimming things.

CATHY. I did six strokes, didn't I Martin? Did I do a width? How many strokes is a length?

How many miles is a swimming pool? I'm going
to take my bronze and silver and gold and diamond.

MARTIN. Is Tommy still wetting the bed?

EDWARD. Don't get angry with him about it.

MARTIN. I just need to go to the launderette
so I've got a spare sheet. Of course I don't get
fucking angry, Eddy, for God's sake. I don't like
to say he is my son but he is my son. I'm surprised
I'm not wetting the bed myself.

CATHY. I don't wet the bed ever. Do you wet
the bed Martin?

MARTIN. No.

CATHY. You said you did.

(BETTY *comes*)

BETTY. I do miss the sun living in England but
today couldn't be more beautiful. You appreciate
the weekend when you're working. Betty's been
at work this week. Cathy. It's terribly tiring Martin.
I don't know how you've done it all these years.
And the money, I feel like a child with the money.
Clive always paid everything but I do understand
it perfectly well. Look Cathy let me show you
my money.

CATHY. I'll count it. Let me count it. What's
that?

BETTY. Five pounds. Five and five is—?

CATHY. One two three—

BETTY. Five and five is ten, and five—

CATHY. If I get it right can I have one?

EDWARD. No you can't.

(CATHY *goes on counting the money*)

BETTY. I never like to say anything, Martin, or you'll think I'm being a mother-in-law.

EDWARD. Which you are.

BETTY. Thank you, Edward, I'm not talking to you. Martin, I think you're being wonderful. Vicky will come back. Just let her stay with Lin till she sorts herself out. It's very nice for a girl to have a friend. I had friends at school, that was very nice. But I'm sure Lin and Edward don't want her with them all the time. I'm not at all shocked that Lin and Edward aren't married and she already has a child, we all know first marriages don't always work out. But really Vicky must be in the way. And poor little Tommy, I hear he doesn't sleep properly and he's had a cough.

MARTIN. No, he's fine, Betty, thank you.

CATHY. My bed's horrible. I want to sleep in the big bed with Lin and Vicky and Eddy and I do get in if I've got a bad dream and my bed's got a bump right in my back. I want to sleep in a tent.

BETTY. Well Tommy has got a nasty cough, Martin, whatever you say.

EDWARD. He's over that. He's got some medicine.

MARTIN. He takes it in Ribena.

BETTY. Well I'm glad to hear it. Look what a lot of money, Cathy, and I sit behind a desk of my own and I answer the telephone and keep the doctor's appointment book and it really is great fun.

CATHY. Can we go camping, Martin, in a tent? We could take the Dead Hand Gang.

BETTY. Not those big boys, Cathy? They're far too big and rough for you. I'm sure mummy doesn't let you play with them, does she Edward? Well I don't know.

(*Ice cream bells*)

CATHY. Ice cream. Martin you promised. I'll have a double ninety nine. No, I'll have a shandy lolly. Betty, you have a shandy lolly and I'll have a lick. No, you have a double ninety nine and I'll have the chocolate.

(MARTIN, CATHY *and* BETTY *go, leaving* EDWARD. GERRY *comes*)

GERRY. Hello, Eddy. I thought I might find you here.

EDWARD. Gerry.

GERRY. Not working today then?

EDWARD. I don't work here anymore.

GERRY. Your mum got you into a dark suit?

EDWARD. No of course not. I'm one of the unemployed. I am working, though. I do housework.

GERRY. Whose wife are you now then?

EDWARD. Nobody's. I'm living with some women.

GERRY. What women?

EDWARD. My sister Vic and her lover. They go out to work and I look after the kids.

GERRY. I thought for a moment you meant you were living with women.

EDWARD. We do sleep together yes.

GERRY. I was passing the park anyway so I thought

I'd look in. I was in the sauna the other night
and I saw someone who looked like you but it
wasn't. I had sex with him anyway.

EDWARD. I do go to the sauna sometimes.

GERRY. I don't think I'd like living with children.
They make a lot of noise don't they?

EDWARD. I tell them to shut up and they shut
up. I wouldn't want to leave them at the moment.

GERRY. Look why don't we go for a meal sometime?

EDWARD. Yes I'd like that. Where are you living
now?

GERRY. Same place.

EDWARD. I'll come round for you about 7:30.

GERRY. Great.

(EDWARD *goes.* HARRY *comes.* HARRY *and* GERRY *pick
each other up and go.* VIC *and* LIN *come*)

VIC. So I said to the professor, I don't think
this is an occasion for invoking the concept of
structural causality—

(BETTY *comes*)

BETTY. I'd like to ask you a question, both of
you. I have a little money from your grandmother.
And the three of you are living in that tiny flat
with two children. I wonder if we could get a
house and all live in it together? It would give
you more room.

VIC. But I'm going to Manchester anyway.

LIN. We'd have a garden, Vicky.

BETTY. You do seem to have such fun all of you.

VIC. I don't want to.

BETTY. I didn't think you would.

LIN. Come on, Vicky, she knows we sleep together, and Eddie.

BETTY. I think I've known for quite a while, but I'm not sure. I don't usually think about it, so I don't know if I know about it or not.

VIC. I don't want to live with my mother.

LIN. Don't think of her as your mother, think of her as Betty.

VIC. But she thinks of herself as my mother.

BETTY. I am your mother.

VIC. But Mummy we don't even like each other.

BETTY. We might begin to.

(CATHY *comes on howling with a nosebleed*)

LIN. Oh Cathy what happened?

BETTY. She's been assaulted.

VIC. It's a nosebleed.

CATHY. Took my ice cream.

LIN. Who did?

CATHY. Took my money.

(MARTIN *comes*)

MARTIN. Is everything all right?

LIN. I thought you were looking after her.

CATHY. They hit me. I can't play. They said I'm a girl.

BETTY. Those dreadful boys, the gang, the Dead Hand.

MARTIN. What do you mean you thought I was looking after her?

LIN. Last I saw her she was with you getting an ice cream. It's your afternoon.

MARTIN. Then she went off to play. She goes off to play. You don't keep an eye on her every minute.

LIN. She doesn't get beaten up when I'm looking after her.

CATHY. Took my money.

MARTIN. Why the hell should I look after your child anyway? I just want Tommy. Why should he live with you and Vicky all week?

LIN. I don't mind if you don't want to look after her but don't say you will and then this happens.

VIC. When I go to Manchester everything's going to be different anyway. Lin's staying here, and you're staying here, we're all going to have to sit down and talk it through.

MARTIN. I'd really enjoy that.

CATHY. Hit me on the face.

LIN. You were the one looking after her and look at her now, that's all.

MARTIN. I've had enough of you telling me.

LIN. Yes you know it all.

MARTIN. Now stop it. I work very hard at not being like this, I could do with some credit.

LIN. OK, you're quite nice, try and enjoy it. Don't make me sorry for you, Martin, it's hard for me too. We've better things to do than quarrel.

I've got to go and sort those little bastards out for a start. Where are they?

CATHY. Don't kill them, mum, hit him. Give them a nosebleed, mum.

(LIN *goes*)

VIC. Tommy's asleep in the pushchair. We'd better wake him up or he won't sleep tonight.

MARTIN. Sometimes I keep him up watching television till he falls asleep on the sofa so I can hold him. Come on, Cathy, we'll get another ice cream.

CATHY. Chocolate sauce and nuts.

VIC. Betty, would you like an ice cream?

BETTY. No thank you, the cold hurts my teeth, but what a nice thought, Vicky, thank you. I'm going to have a quiet sit in the sun.

(VICKY *goes*. MAUD *comes*. GERRY *comes*)

BETTY. I think you used to be Edward's flatmate.

GERRY. You're his mother. He's talked about you.

BETTY. Well never mind. Children are always wrong about their parents. It's a great problem knowing where to live and who to share with. I live by myself just now.

GERRY. Good. So do I. You can do what you like.

BETTY. I don't really know what I like.

GERRY. You'll soon find out.

BETTY. What do you like?

GERRY. Waking up at four in the morning.

BETTY. I like listening to music in bed and sometimes for supper I just have a big piece of bread and dip it in very hot lime pickle. So you don't get lonely by yourself? Perhaps you have a lot of visitors. I've been thinking I should have some visitors, I could give a little dinner party. Would you come? There wouldn't be just bread and lime pickle.

GERRY. Thank you very much.

BETTY. Or don't wait to be asked to dinner. Just drop in informally. I'll give you the address shall I?

MAUD. Betty, I don't like what I see.

BETTY. I don't usually give strange men my address but then you're not a strange man, you're a friend of Edward's.

MAUD. You were such a success as a young girl.

BETTY. I suppose I seem a different generation to you but you are older than Edward. I was married for so many years it's quite hard to know how to get acquainted. But if there isn't a right way to do things you have to invent one.

MAUD. I'm too old for all this fun. (MAUD goes)

BETTY. I always thought my mother was far too old to be attractive but when you get to an age yourself it feels quite different.

GERRY. I think you could be quite attractive.

BETTY. If what?

GERRY. If you stop worrying.

BETTY. I think when I do more about things I worry about them less. So perhaps you could help me do more.

GERRY. I might be going to live with Edward again.

BETTY. That's nice, but I'm rather surprised if he wants to share a flat. He's rather involved with a young woman he lives with, or two young women, I don't understand Edward but never mind.

GERRY. I'm very involved with him.

BETTY. I think Edward did try to tell me once but I didn't listen. So what I'm being told now is that Edward is 'gay', is that right? And you are too. And I've been making rather a fool of myself. But Edward does also sleep with women.

GERRY. He does, yes, I don't.

BETTY. Well people always say it's the mother's fault but I don't intend to start blaming myself. He seems perfectly happy.

GERRY. I could still come and see you.

BETTY. So you could, yes. I'd like that. I've never tried to pick up a man before.

GERRY. Not everyone's gay.

BETTY. No, that's lucky, isn't it.

(GERRY *goes*)

BETTY. I used to think Clive was the one who liked sex. But then I found I missed it. I used to touch myself when I was very little, I thought I'd invented something wonderful. I used to do it to go to sleep with or to cheer myself up, and one day it was raining and I was under the kitchen table, and my mother saw me with my hand under my dress rubbing away, and she dragged me out so quickly I hit my head and it bled and I was sick, and nothing was said, and I never did it again till this year. I thought if Clive wasn't looking at me there wasn't a person there. And one night in bed in my flat I was so frightened I started touching myself. I thought my hand might go through into space. I touched my face, it was there, my arm, my breast, and my hand went down where I thought it shouldn't, and I thought well there is somebody there. It felt very sweet, it was a feeling from very long ago, it was very soft, just barely touching and I felt myself gathering together more and more and I felt angry with Clive and angry with my mother and I went on and on defying them, and there was this vast feeling growing in me and all round me and they couldn't stop me and no one could stop me and I was there and coming and coming! Afterwards I thought I'd betrayed Clive. My mother would kill me. But I felt triumphant because I was a separate person from them. And I cried because I didn't want to be. But I don't cry about it any more. Sometimes I do it three times in one night and it really is great fun.

(JOSHUA *comes*)

JOSHUA. Did Madam hear me wrong? I said you've got legs under that skirt, and more than legs.

(JOSHUA *goes.* CLIVE *comes.*)

CLIVE. You are not that sort of woman Betty. I can't believe you are. I can't feel the same about you as I did. And Africa is to be communist I suppose. I used to be proud to be British. There was a high ideal. I came out onto the verandah and looked at the stars. (CLIVE *goes.* BETTY *from Act I comes.* BETTY *and* BETTY *embrace*)

CLOUD NINE music

THE END

"CLOUD NINE" - COSTUME PLOT

ACT I, SCENE I

BETTY
Black leather "Mary Jones"
Beige knee hose
White batiste petticoat
Beige satin bustle and waist cinch
White camisole
Coral embroidered blouse
Khaki scalloped-hem skirt
Curly brown wig

CLIVE
Black leather boots
Khaki socks
Khaki and ecru striped trousers
White suspenders
Ecru cotton shirt
Black bow tie
White pique vest
Pocket watch and fob
Beige linen jacket
Ecru silk pocket square
Pith helmet

JOSHUA
Printed brown ankle scarf

Sienna and brown print "pant" with leopard
    fur "penis"
White military jacket
Beaded pectoral necklace

MAUD
    Black "character" shoe
    Black tights
    Black taffeta petticoat
    Beige satin bustle and waist cinch
    Purple-lilac lace skirt; lilac bodice with ecru
        lace collar and cuff (brooch)
    Black hair piece with "doiley"
    Amethyst pendant earrings
    Powder blue lace shawl

ELLEN
    Black high-buttoned show
Black tights
    Beige satin bustle
    White camisole
    White blouse
    White mop cap
    White half apron
    Black faille skirt

EDWARD
    Navy boots
    Navy blue socks
    Blue-grey knicers
    Blue-grey sailor top
    Red wig
    Gold-rimmed glasses

VICTORIA
   Rose print dress
   White bloomers
   White anklets
   Black high-button shoes

HARRY BAGLEY
   Grey socks
   Brown lace-up boots
   Khaki jodphurs
   Ecru silk shirt
   Brown saber belt
   Ochre leather gloves
   Khaki bush jacket
   Pith helmet
   Moustache

MRS. SAUNDERS (The Same Actress who Plays Ellen)
   Take off mop cap and apron, put on:
      Banana riding jacket
      Top hat with snood
      Banana riding gloves with black trim

* All the characters who appear in the prologue with the exception of Maud, who does not wear her shawl

ACT I, SCENE 2
   All characters appearing in this scene wear the same costumes as in Act I, Scene I, with the exception of Harry Bagley, who removes his jacket, hat and gloves, and Maud, who removes her shawl.

Harry does put his jacket back on after his exit
on P.   Clive after his exit on P.   removes
his hat.

ACT I, SCENE 3
Clive removes his jacket, and later on P.   he
puts it back on. Harry Bagley removes his jacket
after his exit on P.

ACT I, SCENE 4
Harry Bagley wears his bush jacket.

ACT I, SCENE 5
Ellen enters wearing an embroidered table veil
in ecru. Harry Bagley changes into a formal
military jacket with epaulettes. Clive wears a
white baldric trimmed in gold. Ellen exits on
P. and changes into Mrs. Saunders. Mrs. Saunders
exits on P.   and returns as Ellen with her veil.

ACT II, SCENE 1
CATHY
Black Cloth "Mary Jones"
Pink ankle socks
Pink panties with ruffles
Pink short-sleeved dress
Black plaited wig
Pink shoulder bag of plastic

VICTORIA
Red suede flats with ankle strap
Dark socks

Blue jeans with black belt
Green silk blouse
Red appliqued car coat

LIN

Black cowboy boots
Cotton socks
Faded denim jeans, black belt
White sweat shirt
Black 40's dress suit jacket
Hair combs

LIN

Black cowboy boots
Cotton socks
Faded denim jeans, black belt
White sweat shirt
Black 40's dress suit jacket
Hair combs

CATHY

exits on P.   and returns on the same page
wearing a red and purple satin baseball jacket
over her above-mentioned costume.

EDWARD

Black rubber fireman's boots
Khaki socks
White and brown pinstripe shirt
Grey canvas overalls
Charcola grey coat
Charcoal grey cap
Bandana blue and white dots

White cotton knit gloves in pocket of coat
Gold rimmed glasses

BETTY
Silver grey pumps
Nude panty hose
Off-white full slip
Ecru cotton blouse
Grey tweed silk suit (skirt, jacket)
Crystal necklace
Brown houndstooth cape
Matching pill box hat
Pearl clip-button earrings
Brown leather purse
Brown suede gloves

LIN
Brown houndstooth cape
Matching pillbox hat
Pearl clip-button earrings
Brown leather purse
Brown suede gloves

LIN
puts purple wool muffler on Cathy on P.
that has been preset at the top of Act II.

CATHY
exits on P.   and removes purple and red satin
jacket and purple muffler.

LIN
exits on P.   and removes dress suit jacket
(black) and puts on grey flannel shirt.

VICTORIA
exits on P.   removes red car coat and puts
on beige acrylic cardigan.

EDWARD
enters at the top of P.   and removes hat.

GERRY
    Black high jump sneakers
    Socks
    Black corduroy jeans
    Purple sleeveless sweat shirt
    Black baseball jacket-silver sleeves

MARTIN
    Camel-colored loafers
    Grey socks
    Blue denim painters jeans
    Khaki cotton crew-necked sweater
    Khaki and beige checked sport coat
    Horn-rimmed glasses

BETTY
BETTY, after her exit on P.   removes her
cape and hat and changes her blouse to a beige
silk one with a bow.

    MARTIN, after his exit on P.   removes his
    sport coat, sweater and glasses and puts on
    a blue sport shirt.

CATHY, after her exit on P.   removes her
wig, dress and shoulder bag; the actor then dresses

for BILL in olive fatigue soldier suit (jacket and
.pants) and a black wool private's beret.

LIN, after her exit on P.   removes her gray
flannel shirt.

EDWARD, enters on P.   wearing topsiders,
faded denim jeans, pale blue and white polka
dot shirt and a faded denim jacket.

VICTORIA, after her exit on P.   , removes her
sweater and enters on P.   with her blouse sleev
es   pushed up.

EDWARD, after his exit on P.   overdresses
for EDWARD I in sailor top, glasses and wig.

EDWARD, after his exit on P.   removes light
blue polka dot shirt and changes to a gingham
checked one in blue and white.

BILL, THE SOLDIER, after his exit on P.   removes
fatigue suit and beret and changes back to CATHY
black plaited wig, pink dress, and pink shoulder
bag.

LIN, after her exit on P.   puts on a navy
blue man's vest, and combs her hair into a
high pony tail.

EDWARD I, after his exit on P.   removes
his sailor top, wig and glasses, and as Victoria
knots her blouse mid-driff style.

MARTIN, after his exit on P.   overdresses
into Harry Bagley: khaki pleated trousers, military dress jacket, pith helmet, and moustache.

HARRY, after his exit on P.   removes all
above-mentioned costumes.

GERRY, after his exit on P.   removes his
baseball jacket.

EDWARD II, after his exit on P.   changes
into his costume for Clive (see pages 1 and
2.)

LIN, after her exit on P.   removes her white
sweat shirt and vest and overdresses as Maud
into bodice, skirt and wig.

VICTORIA, after her exit on P.   overdresses
into Edward I: sailor top, knickers, wig, glasses
and black high-buttoned shoes with velcro.

MARTIN, after his exit, on P.   overdresses
into Harry Bagley, only now he wears khaki
buch jacket.

CATHY, after her exit on P.   changes into
Joshua.

GERRY, after his exit on P.   , overdresses into
Act I Betty.

BETTY II takes curtain call as herself.

BETTY II, after her exit on P.   overdresses into Mrs. Saunders

ALL ACTORS take bows in Act I costumes.

MRS SAUNDERS removes hat anc hacket and puts on mop cap and apron for Ellen.

ALL undressed actors remove Act I costumes for bows as Act II characters.

JOSHUA back into Cathy dress, wig and shoes.

CLIVE puts on Edward's gardeners' coat

MAUD puts on Lin's white sweat shirt.

ACT ONE PRESENT

Book of poetry (Betty) .... **SR**

Drum with strap (Joshua) .... **SR**

Pitch Pipe (Ellen) .... **SL**

Victoria, the doll (Maud) .... **SR**

Wicker tray and wooden glass
with bamboo straw (Joshua) .... **SR**

Riding crop (Clive) .... **Rear of House**

Two rifles with straps (Joshua and
Clive) .... **On set**

Short riding crop (Harry) .... **Personal**

Victorian doll (Edward) .... **SR**

Riding crop and binoculars
(Mrs. Saunders) .... **Rear of House**

Picnic hamper, ground cloth, napkin,
five wooden goblets, a wicker fan,
and pitch pipe .... **SR**

Champagne bottle (Clive) .... **SR**

Parasol (Maud) .... **SL**

Ball (Ellen) .... **SR**

Crystal beads (Edward) .... **SR**

Wicker tray with wooden goblets
from hamper (Joshua) .... **SR**

Wedding bouquet (Ellen) .... **SR**

Wedding cake on pedestal, the cake
is three-tiered (Edward) .... **SR**

Knife on wicker tray with fruit
(Joshua) .... **SR**

Six to seven Union Jacks which have
been strung together; graduating

in size from six to twelve inches.

This is Harry's conjuring trick .... SL
Wooden rifle (Joshua) .... SR
Letter (Clive) .... SR
Victorian hand bag with
    ointment jar (Maud) .... SL
Gourd rattle .... SL
Gloves (Clive) .... Rear of House

ACT TWO PRESENT
Book, handbag (Victoria) .... SR
Yellow bouncing ball (Cathy) .... SR
Finger-painting equipment, rag
    and pad .... SL Bench
Tote bag containing apron, portable
    radio and scarf .... SL Bench
Garden shears (Edward) .... Rear aof House
Earrings, beads from Act I, hat,
    gloves, purse with tissue, English
    money, coins, change purse, candies,
    pad and pencil (Betty) .... Personal
Filled grocery bag (Edward) .... SR
Cap gun on holster (Cathy) .... Personal
Chianti bottle (Edward) .... SR
Cigarettes (Martin) .... SL
Gym bag with "swimming stuff"
    (Edward) .... SL
Edward's doll from Act I (Edward) .... SR
Lunch bag with sandwich and apple
    Gerry) .... Rear of House
Tray and goblets from Act I (Joshua) .... SR
Pepsi-cola can (Gerry) .... SR
Stage blood (Cathy) .... Rear of House

TAPED CLOUD 9 SOUND EFFECTS NYC

ACT I — AMBIANCE — JUNGLE BIRDS (Continuous except during flogging scene — Iiii)

Ii

1. — Jungle Bird Call — Top of show
2. — Drums — End of "Come Gather" Song
3. — Jungle Bird Call — Exit Maud, "Think I am *strong enough*"
4. — Horse neighs into Horses Gallop — Exit of Harry & Joshua, end of scene

Iii

5. — Champagne Cork Popping — Clive opens champagne

Iiii

6. — "Africana" music — End scene EDWARD: "don't *touch me*" thru Joshua's story Iiv until "of course it's not true".

Iiv

7. — Drumming — End scene CLIVE: "get out of *my sight*" thru Joshua's business w/doll until Maud's entrance

Iv

8. — Drumming — Builds from CLIVE: "cut *the cake*" until end of scene.
9. — Gunshots to CLOUD 9 Music (Fast) — CLIVE: "peace and joy and *bliss*".

ACT II — AMBIANCE — (1) PARK BIRDS (except GERRY's monologue IIii, all of IIiii, BETTY's monologue, end of show) **(2) HOOT OWLS** (during IIiii, except BILL's monologue)

10. — Radio Announcement to — Top of Act CLOUD 9 Music (Fast)
11. — CLOUD NINE Music (Fast) — End IIi — LIN: "You'd enjoy *it*".
12. — CLOUD NINE Music (Flute) — End IIii — EDW: "Think I'm a *lesbian*" thru IIiii until LIN: "and *blood*".
13. — CLOUD NINE Music(Slow) — End IIiii GERRY: "never let them stay the *night*." until IIiv

IIiv

14. — Ice Cream Bells — BETTY: "I don't know"
15. — CLOUD NINE Music (Flute) — GERRY: "*Hello, Eddy*" thru GERRY "Great"
16. — "Africana" Music — BETTY: "a quiet sit in the *sun*" thru scene til Maud's exit
17. — CLOUD 9 Music (Slow) — BETTY: (Monologue), "coming and *coming*", thru end of show.
18. — CLOUD 9 Music (Fast) — Curtain Call.

110

Other Publications for Your Interest

AGNES OF GOD
(LITTLE THEATRE—DRAMA)

By JOHN PIELMEIER

3 women—1 set (bare stage)

Doctor Martha Livingstone, a court-appointed psychiatrist, is asked to determine the sanity of a young nun accused of murdering her own baby. Mother Miriam Ruth, the nun's superior, seems bent on protecting Sister Agnes from the doctor, and Livingstone's suspicions are immediately aroused. In searching for solutions to various mysteries (who killed the baby? Who fathered the child?) Livingstone forces all three women, herself included, to face some harsh realities in their own lives, and to re-examine the meaning of faith and the commitment of love. "Riveting, powerful, electrifying new drama . . . three of the most magnificent performances you will see this year on any stage anywhere . . . the dialogue crackles."—Rex Reed, N.Y. Daily News. ". . . outstanding play . . . deals intelligently with questions of religion and psychology."—Mel Gussow, N.Y. Times. ". . . unquestionably blindingly theatrical . . . cleverly executed blood and guts evening in the theatre . . . three sensationally powered performances calculated to wring your withers."—Clive Barnes, N.Y. Post.   (#236)

(Posters available)

COME BACK TO THE 5 & DIME, JIMMY DEAN, JIMMY DEAN
(ADVANCED GROUPS—DRAMA)

By ED GRACZYK

1 man, 8 women—Interior

In a small-town dime store in West Texas, the Disciples of James Dean gather for their twentieth reunion. Now a gaggle of middle-aged women, the Disciples were teenagers when Dean filmed "Giant" two decades ago in nearby Marfa. One of them, an extra in the film, has a child whom she says was conceived by Dean on the "Giant" set; the child is the Jimmy Dean of the title. The ladies' reminiscences mingle with flash-backs to their youth; then the arrival of a stunning and momentarily unrecognized woman sets off a series of confrontations that upset their self-deceptions and expose their well-hidden disappointments. "Full of homespun humor . . . surefire comic gems."—N.Y. Post. "Captures convincingly the atmosphere of the 1950s."—Women's Wear Daily.   (#5147)

Other Publications for Your Interest

A WEEKEND NEAR MADISON
(LITTLE THEATRE—COMIC DRAMA)
By KATHLEEN TOLAN

2 men, 3 women—Interior

This recent hit from the famed Actors Theatre of Louisville, a terrific ensemble play about male-female relationships in the 80's, was praised by *Newsweek* as "warm, vital, glowing . . . full of wise ironies and unsentimental hopes". The story concerns a weekend reunion of old college friends now in their early thirties. The occasion is the visit of Vanessa, the queen bee of the group, who is now the leader of a lesbian/feminist rock band. Vanessa arrives at the home of an old friend who is now a psychiatrist hand in hand with her naif-like lover, who also plays in the band. Also on hand are the psychiatrist's wife, a novelist suffering from writer's block; and his brother, who was once Vanessa's lover and who still loves her. In the course of the weekend, Vanessa reveals that she and her lover desperately want to have a child—and she tries to persuade her former male lover to father it, not understanding that he might have some feelings about the whole thing. *Time Magazine* heard "the unmistakable cry of an infant hit . . . Playwright Tolan's work radiates promise and achievement." (#25051)

PASTORALE
(LITTLE THEATRE—COMEDY)
By DEBORAH EISENBERG

3 men, 4 women—Interior
(plus 1 or 2 bit parts and 3 optional extras)

"Deborah Eisenberg is one of the freshest and funniest voices in some seasons."—Newsweek. Somewhere out in the country Melanie has rented a house and in the living room she, her friend Rachel who came for a weekend but forgets to leave, and their school friend Steve (all in their mid-20s) spend nearly a year meandering through a mental landscape including such concerns as phobias, friendship, work, sex, slovenliness and epistemology. Other people happen by: Steve's young girlfriend Celia, the virtuous and annoying Edie, a man who Melanie has picked up in a bar, and a couple who appear during an intense conversation and observe the sofa is on fire. The lives of the three friends inevitably proceed and eventually draw them, the better prepared perhaps by their months on the sofa, in separate directions. "The most original, funniest new comic voice to be heard in New York theater since Beth Henley's 'Crimes of the Heart.'"—N.Y. Times. "A very funny, stylish comedy."—The New Yorker. "Wacky charm and wayward wit."—New York Magazine. "Delightful."—N.Y. Post. "Uproarious . . . the play is a world unto itself, and it spins."—N.Y. Sunday Times. (#18016)